THE BLUE MOON DAY

Alison Prince was born in Beckenham, Kent, of a Scottish mother and Yorkshire father. She won a scholarship to the Slade School of Fine Art and began a teaching career on leaving college, but soon moved into freelance writing and illustration. For eight years she ran a small farm in Suffolk, then moved to a village near Stamford, in Lincolnshire. She now lives in Scotland, on the Isle of Arran. She has three grown-up children.

Other books by Alison Prince include *A Job For Merv* and *The Type One Super Robot*. *How's Business* is also available in Piper.

GW01066357

Also by Alison Prince in Piper

How's Business

Alison Prince

THE BLUE MOON DAY

and other stories

With illustrations by the author

Piper Books

First published 1988 by Marilyn Malin Books
in association with André Deutsch Limited

This edition published 1990 by
Pan Books Ltd, Cavaye Place, London SW10 9PG

9 8 7 6 5 4 3 2 1

Text and illustration © 1988 Alison Prince

ISBN 0 330 32259 6

Printed in Great Britain by
Richard Clay Ltd, Bungay, Suffolk

Contents

The Blue Moon Day 7

The Deep Hole Day 55

The Sorting-out Day 85

The Two-Day 119

The Blue Moon Day

Dave's mother had gone away for a week, on business, she said. So Dave was staying with his grandmother, Primrose.

Dave was not pleased. He felt that he was much too old to be parked with a granny. 'I could look after myself,' he grumbled as he dumped his bag on Primrose's kitchen floor. 'I'm almost grown up. I wish I *was* grown up,' he added, 'then I'*d* be away on business, too. Only I'd have a really decent car, not like that old Renault 4 of Mum's. And I'd have a telephone in it.'

'Personally,' said Primrose, 'I think all that is very over-rated. Come and look at my beautiful garden.'

Dave looked. The garden seemed to be mostly weeds. Privately, he thought it was a mess. 'I wish wishes came true,' he said.

Primrose seemed to know what he was thinking. 'It's a *wild* garden,' she explained. 'I like it that way. And wishes do come true if you wait long enough.'

'I don't want to wait,' said Dave. 'I want my wishes to come true *now*.' He knew he was being unreasonable, but he didn't care.

Primrose laughed. 'That only happens once in a blue moon,' she said.

'Huh,' said Dave gloomily. 'And when's that?'

'Not often,' said Primrose.

That night, Dave lay awake, staring crossly out of the window while Primrose played something very old-fashioned on the piano downstairs. There had been nothing worth watching on television. A full moon hung in the sky behind the dark trees, round and brilliant, and the longer Dave stared at it, the more he began to feel that it was a very odd colour. He shut his eyes for a moment, then looked at it again, suspiciously. There was no doubt about it. The moon was a pale, clear blue. Dave laughed. 'Come on, then,' he said to it. 'Do your stuff. *I wish I was grown up.*' He held his arms out to see if they were getting any bigger but, as he had expected, they weren't.

'Huh!' said Dave again, and pulled the curtains across to shut out the mocking face of the pale-blue moon. Then he turned on his side and went to sleep.

In the morning, Dave woke up feeling terribly uncomfortable. His pyjamas seemed to be throttling him. He pushed the bedclothes back to see what had happened — and stared at his feet in astonishment. They were huge. And his legs were huge, too, long and thick and hairy, with the too-small pyjamas cutting grooves in

8

their calves. His arms were hairy as well, gripped tightly round the elbows by the pyjama sleeves.

Dave got up, and found that his head was level with the top of the mirror over the washbasin. Stooping a little, he peered at his reflected face, which was large and stubbly-chinned. He reached out to touch the glass, wondering if the face really was his own, and connected with his reflected finger.

'It *is* me,' said Dave aloud. His voice was gruff, and the lips of his reflection moved as he spoke. His wish had come true. He was grown up.

He sat down on his bed again, feeling embarrassed. This was crazy. It couldn't have happened. Perhaps he was dreaming, he thought. Then he heard Primrose go down the stairs to the kitchen. Was she in the dream, too? Pinch yourself, they said. He dug his nails hard into the hairy skin of his arm and heard his deep voice say, 'Ow!' as the sharp pain made itself felt.

Dave decided to go down and see Primrose. If he was just imagining all this, she would greet him without surprise, as his usual self. He started to struggle out of the tight pyjamas. Then he stopped, struck by a new thought. The tee shirt and jeans he had worn yesterday would be far too small. All the clothes he had would be too small.

Dave managed to pull on a pair of underpants which stretched obligingly, then hunted in desperation in the wardrobe for any clothes which might have belonged to his long-dead grandfather. There were none, but he found a pair of flowered cotton trousers and a kind of shirt which he seemed to remember seeing on Primrose. He put them on, and pushed his feet into a pair of Indian sandals. Then he went downstairs.

His grandmother was in the kitchen, doing her yoga. She gazed at Dave and said, 'Good morning. Are you a burglar?'

'No,' said Dave in his new, deep voice. 'I thought all that stuff about the blue moon was rubbish, but it wasn't. I've grown up.'

'Goodness,' said Primrose. 'So you're Dave. Well, well. What would you like for breakfast? Muesli and chopped banana?'

'Peanut butter on toast,' said Dave rather sulkily. 'Please.' He felt that his grandmother might have been a little more excited.

'You look awfully funny in those clothes,' said Primrose when she put the toast and a glass of apple juice on the table. 'Can't you wish for some more suitable ones?'

'It's daytime now,' Dave pointed out. 'The blue moon's gone.'

Primrose looked out of the window. 'It hasn't,' she said. 'It's as large as life. Larger.'

She was right. The full moon hung above the trees as it had done last night, but now it was a brighter blue than the blue sky.

Staring at it, Dave forgot about feeling silly. 'I wish for some really posh clothes,' he said. And instantly, he found himself dressed in a tail coat and striped trousers, with a starched white shirt, elegantly ruffled, and a rose-coloured velvet bow tie.

Primrose laughed so much that she nearly choked on her camomile tea.

Dave turned pinker than his tie and said, 'I wish for some *un*posh clothes!' At once, he was wearing a boiler suit and a pair of knobbly boots with metal toe-caps.

'No, *no*!' said Dave, exasperated. 'I wish for just *ordinary* clothes!'

This time he was in a brown jacket, with brown trousers and brown suede shoes.

'It's no good,' said Primrose, wiping her eyes. 'You'll have to know exactly what you want before you wish. You really can't deal in these generalities. Eat your toast, it's getting cold.'

'Don't you want a wish?' asked Dave as he munched.

'Oh, no,' said Primrose. 'I wouldn't dare. You never know what might happen. And anyway, I like things as they are.'

Dave shrugged. It was tempting to do something wild, like turning himself into a space rocket, but his new, grown-up self frowned upon such frivolity. Wishes were not to be wasted on silliness.

Primrose sipped her tea. 'Are you grown up for always?' she enquired. 'Or is it just for today?'

'I don't know,' Dave admitted. The possibilities were endless. 'Can I have some more toast?'

'Help yourself,' said Primrose.

Dave cut two slices of bread and dropped them into the toaster. The knife seemed very small in his big hand. Suddenly, grown up or not, he felt a surge of wild excitement. 'I'm going to have an amazing day!' he said.

'I'm sure you are,' said Primrose.

With tremendous self-control, Dave refrained from doing anything amazing until after he had helped with the washing-up. Then he said, 'Right. Now, first of all, I wish for a large car, with a telephone in it.'

And there it was.

'Not in the kitchen!' shrieked Primrose, flattened between the car and the Aga.

'Outside,' said Dave quickly. When the car had vanished from the kitchen he opened the back door and went out to look at it in the garden.

'It's squashing my borage,' said Primrose fretfully.

'Never mind,' said Dave. 'I'll wish it unsquashed afterwards.' He opened the car's door and got into the driving seat. There was a wonderful smell of leather, and the glossy walnut dashboard held a vast array of dials, all looking quietly efficient behind their mysterious grey smoked glass. Dave stared at them in frustration. 'I wish I knew how to drive,' he said — and at once, it was all clear to him. He laughed with delight, and started the engine.

'Now, Dave, wait a minute,' said Primrose. 'What are you going to do?'

'Business,' said Dave. 'All grown-ups have business.'

'I don't,' said Primrose.

Dave ignored this. 'I wish for business,' he said firmly, and a black briefcase appeared on the back seat of the car. There was a pink newspaper beside him, and a voice came from the radio telephone mounted on the dash. 'Sue from Megabiz here, sir,' it said. 'You won't forget the meeting with Mr Purse this morning, will you?'

Dave felt obscurely worried, despite his excitement. 'I must go,' he said.

'I think you are making a mistake,' said Primrose.

But Dave was already driving the car across the garden towards the gate. He just managed to wave to Primrose and cast a hasty wish in the direction of the borage before he was out on the road, heading towards the town.

This is wonderful, Dave said to himself as the big car sped along, up and down hills, past fields and woods and through villages. This is what being grown up is all about. He hooted the horn and flashed the lights and made the electric windows go up and down. 'Sue from Megabiz again, sir,' said the voice from the telephone. 'Are you on your way? You mustn't be late for Mr Purse.'

'I'm being as quick as I can,' said Dave with a trace of irritation. He had come up behind a tractor pulling a trailer laden with hay, and the road was so twisty that

17

he could not overtake. 'He can only spare you five minutes,' said Sue from Megabiz.

'All *right*,' snapped Dave. Then he realized that there was no need to creep along behind a tractor if he didn't want to. 'I wish I was at the place I'm going to,' he said.

The noise of traffic was deafening. Dave was parked in a crowded street outside a huge building with MEGABIZ in vast gold letters above the door.

'Can't stop here, sir,' said a traffic warden.

'But I've got to see this man called Mr Purse,' said Dave. 'I'll only be five minutes, honest.'

'Oh, yes?' said the traffic warden. 'I wish I had a tenner for every motorist who's told me that.'

'I wish you had, too,' said Dave generously.

The warden was instantly showered with ten-pound notes. Dave retrieved his newspaper and his briefcase from the car and said, 'I wish this car would disappear.' After all, he thought, he could easily wish it back later.

The traffic warden was too busy with his armfuls of money to notice that the car had gone, but an Indian gentleman rushed up to Dave and shook him by the hand excitedly. 'Most honoured sir,' he said, 'congratulations! My name is Mr Sen, magician and conjuror, children's parties a speciality. Here is my card.' He handed Dave a rather dog-eared small card, which Dave put in his pocket. 'But I am not often seeing magic of this *size*,' Mr Sen rushed on. 'A whole magnificent car!' He put his hand on Dave's sleeve confidentially. 'Tell me,' he said. 'As one professional to another — where did you put it?'

19

'I don't know,' Dave confessed. 'It just — went.'

Mr Sen clasped his hands together in rapture and said, 'Oh, how I wish I could do that!'

He seemed a nice man, Dave thought. And one should not be selfish. 'Okay,' he said easily. 'I wish you could make cars disappear. Go on — try it.'

Mr Sen approached a dilapidated Mini and waved his hand at it. 'Vanish!' he commanded — and it did. With a shriek of delight, he went on down the street and caused the disappearance of a delivery van, a Rolls Royce and six assorted Fords.

This time, the traffic warden did notice. He was struggling with a lot of people who had crowded round him, demanding to know how they could have ten-pound notes as well, but he shouted, 'Oy! Those cars had got parking tickets on!'

'Even more wonderful!' chortled Mr Sen. 'I am causing the vanishing of parking tickets! And also of stuffed dogs with wobbly heads and dangling furry dice! Thank you, thank you, most excellent sir! With this new trick I shall be on television!' And he shook Dave's hand again.

The people surrounding the traffic warden were almost knocking him off his feet, shouting at each other and trying to grab ten-pound notes.

'It was him that did it!' cried the warden desperately, pointing at Dave. 'He can do anything. You ask him!'

The crowd rushed at Dave, tugging at his jacket and trying to snatch his briefcase, shouting for money and wishes. This was not fun at all, Dave thought as they pushed him about. And besides, it suddenly seemed a long time since his toast and peanut butter. 'I wish I was in a cafe — not near here,' he said quickly.

The cafe was very crowded. 'Oh dear,' Dave murmured to himself. 'I wish there was somewhere to sit.'

He had not meant it as a wish that was supposed to come true, but two lorry-drivers instantly disappeared from their table in front of him, and he was sitting in their place.

''Ere!' said a remaining lorry-driver. 'What's going on? Where's Len and Fred? And who the heck are you?'

'Never seen nothing like it,' said his mate, and prodded Dave in the chest. 'I don't know what you're playing at,' he said, 'but we want Len and Fred back. Now.'

Dave stood up and shuffled out of the way in case he should be squashed by Len and Fred when they reappeared. 'Sorry,' he said. 'Mistake.' Then he wished the drivers back in their places and hastily wished himself elsewhere — with plenty of room.

'Good morning, sir,' said the waiter, flicking the table cloth with a white napkin. 'I didn't see you come in. I'm afraid we don't start serving lunch until twelve. Some coffee for you, sir?'

'I'm not keen on coffee,' said Dave. 'Can I have beans on toast and a glass of Coke?'

The waiter looked distasteful. 'This is a high-class establishment, sir,' he said. 'We do not serve beans on toast.'

Dave wondered whether to try somewhere else — but it seemed difficult to get wishes absolutely right, and he was hungry. 'I wish for beans on toast,' he said obstinately. 'And Coke.'

The waiter gasped as a steaming plateful arrived in front of Dave, with a glass of Coke beside it. 'I shall fetch the manager,' he said.

'Do,' said Dave, tucking in.

The waiter came back with the manager and they both began to protest very loudly about customers bringing their own food. Dave sighed and said, 'I do wish you'd shut up.' Then he finished his beans in perfect silence, while the waiter and the manager turned all sorts of colours as they struggled, without success, to speak.

An odd bleeping noise was coming from the top pocket of Dave's brown jacket. He discovered a slim metal box with a button on it, which he pressed experimentally. 'Sue from Megabiz, sir,' said the familiar voice, sounding agitated. 'In another few minutes you will be *late* for your meeting with Mr Purse.'

'Oh,' said Dave. 'All right. I'll be there in a minute.'

'I'll tell him,' said the voice. 'But do be quick.'

Dave mopped up the last of his beans, wondering why he felt so worried. Perhaps this was a side-effect of being grown up, he thought. Mr Purse was obviously very important. He finished his Coke, wished the plate and glass to disappear, then walked out of the restaurant, followed by the furious but still speechless waiter and manager.

Down the street, a commotion was going on. A police car raced past with its light flashing and its siren blaring, but as it approached the crowd of shouting, struggling people, it vanished, leaving two startled policemen sitting in the road. Mr Sen was obviously still making cars disappear. Dave felt guilty. He should have realized that people wouldn't like it — specially if they happened to be the owners of the cars. He would have to do something about it.

Followed by the frantic waiter and the restaurant manager, Dave made his way towards the crowd, thinking hard. He was not sure how the wish-granting system worked. If he simply wished the disappeared cars back in their places, there was a risk that they might arrive on top of cars which had been parked there since. He began to feel seriously anxious.

Suddenly, Dave's arms were grabbed from behind. His briefcase was snatched from his hand and his pink newspaper fell on the pavement. He gasped with terror — then found that he had been seized, not by muggers, but by two large policemen.

'We have reason to believe,' said one of them, 'that you are involved in the mass disappearance of cars from this area.'

'That's him,' agreed a man with a ten-pound note clutched in his fist. 'Saw him with my own eyes, I did. Him and that chap in the turban.'

'I was just coming to sort it out,' protested Dave. He saw that Mr Sen, too, was being firmly held by a group of policemen. A large black van approached down the street with the blue light on its roof flashing, but Mr Sen was clearly unrepentant and the van in its turn disappeared, leaving the squad of policemen it had contained sprawling untidily in the road.

The policemen picked themselves up and came running across to help bundle Dave and Mr Sen along to the police station, where they were marched up the steps into a bare room in which an officer with a lot of shiny buttons on his uniform was sitting behind a table. Quite a big crowd came in with Dave and Mr Sen and the policemen, and they were all talking at once — except for the waiter and the manager, who just made faces and waved their arms.

'I am wishing to speak to my colleague,' insisted Mr Sen, trying to make his way towards Dave. 'I am needing to know the second secret of this trick — how to make the cars visible again.'

'That is what we are all needing to know,' said the man with shiny buttons grimly.

Everyone looked at Dave, and an expectant silence fell, in which a high-pitched bleeping sound could be heard. It came from Dave's pocket. 'I'm awfully sorry,'

Dave whispered to it, 'but I'm in a police station.' The situation was somewhat embarrassing. He wondered whether to wish himself at Megabiz, but decided that it wouldn't be fair to leave Mr Sen in the lurch.

'Mr Purse is extremely displeased,' said the voice from Dave's pocket.

A young policeman tittered and said, 'He's not the only one,' then blushed as the man with the buttons gave him a stony look.

Dave did his very best to explain. He left out the business about the blue moon day and about growing up so suddenly, because he could see that they wouldn't believe it, but he had to tell them about wishes coming true. He knew as he was talking that it all sounded ridiculous, but he struggled on. 'I *can* make the cars appear again,' he assured them earnestly, 'only I've got to be careful where they arrive. I need a big open space. And I don't know where there is one.'

'There's always the park,' suggested the young policeman helpfully, and was glared at again by the man with the buttons.

'All right,' said Dave desperately. 'I wish that Mr Sen can't make cars disappear any more, and I wish all the cars that went are back in the park safely. Oh — and I wish these two gentlemen can talk again.'

The waiter and the manager began to babble about beans on toast, but they were not heard in the general pandemonium as the policemen roared with laughter at

28

the idea of wishes coming true and Mr Sen protested at the loss of the wonderful trick.

'Gibberish,' said the man with shiny buttons. 'Absolute gibberish. Take these two away and lock them up. And send for a psychiatrist.'

Locked in a cell in the deepest bowels of the police station, Dave looked at Mr Sen sadly. 'I really am sorry about the cars,' he said.

Mr Sen had stopped protesting. He shrugged and said, 'I am really not minding too much. I am thinking that this modern magic is basically unreliable. Like electricity, you see. Very good when it is working, no good at all when it is not. I am really preferring the traditional magic. If I had a rope and a penny whistle, for example, I could be out of here in a trice.'

'Really?' said Dave, interested. 'Well, that seems harmless enough. I wish you had them.'

A coil of thick rope instantly appeared on the floor in front of Mr Sen, and there was a penny whistle between his long fingers. He smiled, and began to play a strange, wavering tune.

Slowly, the rope uncurled. One end of it reared up into the air like the head end of a snake, its tip bent over a little as if it was listening to Mr Sen. Up and up it went, swaying in time to the music. When it met the ceiling, it went through it as though the hard white surface was nothing but mist. The remaining coil of rope was steadily unwinding as it travelled upwards. Mr Sen, still playing one-handedly on his penny whistle, took hold of the rope and tucked his foot round it as he started to rise. The last Dave saw of him as he disappeared through the white mist of the ceiling was his rather dilapidated trainers gripping the last few inches of the rope. Then he was gone.

Dave was alone in the cell. He stared at the ceiling, now hard and white again, and felt an even worse anxiety creep into his mind. How could he possibly explain to the police where Mr Sen had gone? The bleeper in his pocket gave a preliminary squeak, and Dave felt a rush of blood to the head. All this nagging and bother was not what he had wished for. 'Sue from —' began the bleeper. Dave put his finger on the button. 'All *right*!' he shouted. 'I'm just coming!' The police would have to look after their own problems. He sighed, and added aloud, 'I wish I was at Megabiz.'

He walked up the flight of steps to the big building and was pounced on by a girl in a neat blouse and skirt as soon as he got through the revolving door. '*There* you are!' she said. 'Where have you *been*?'

Dave knew the voice. 'Hello, Sue,' he said wearily. 'Sorry I'm late. A friend of mine had a little trouble with the police.' Somehow, he did not like to tell her he had been arrested.

Sue was staring at his brown jacket and trousers and his suede shoes. 'I hope you won't think I'm being personal, sir,' she said, 'but you seem to be wearing your weekend clothes. And have you shaved today?'

Dave ran his hand over his rough chin. 'I didn't think of it,' he admitted. He glanced down at himself. His jacket had a missing button and one of the pockets had been half torn off, probably by the people wanting ten-pound notes.

'I wish I looked right for seeing Mr Purse,' he said without much interest, and was immediately smooth-chinned and neatly brushed, in a dark suit.

Sue gave a gasp of astonishment. 'Oh, I wish I could do that!' she said. 'Fancy being able to look exactly the way you wanted to, just like that! How *wonderful*!'

Dave hesitated. Surely, he thought, it couldn't do anyone any harm if Sue looked the way she liked? He smiled at her. 'All right,' he said. 'I wish that you can look exactly the way you want to. Go on — try it.'

Sue immediately looked like a Royal person on a
State visit, then like a motor-biker, then like an old-
fashioned film star.

Shrieking with excitement, she ran down the corridor
scattering sequins and feathers and flung open the door
of a huge room where dozens of typists typed. 'Look!'
she cried. 'Isn't it amazing! Mr Moon can make wishes
come true!'

Dave wanted to point out that his name was actually Parker, but all the typists had leapt up and were rushing at him screaming that they wanted to look as they liked, too. The bedlam was so great that other doors opened and frowning people came out, demanding to know what was going on. Sue was changing from outfit to outfit and hairstyle to hairstyle so fast that it made Dave feel dizzy. The typists went on screaming and the people from the other offices quickly became excited as well. A man seized Dave by the arm and said, 'Just give me one wish, that's all. Just one.'

'What is it?' shouted Dave in the rising uproar.

'A horse,' said the man urgently. 'My little girl wants a horse. She pesters the life out of me. Go on — you can do it.'

'Oh, all right,' said Dave, too tired to argue. 'I wish you had a horse.' An enormous carthorse with hairy legs and jingling harness promptly appeared, and the man gazed at it doubtfully. 'It's a bit big,' he said. 'I was thinking more of a pony, really.'

As soon as people saw the horse, they rushed at Dave, demanding three-piece suites and Aston Martins and double glazing, clutching at his new dark clothes and shaking him and shouting in his face. Suddenly he felt he could not stand it any longer. 'For goodness' sake!' he yelled. 'Have whatever you like, only leave me alone! I wish you can all have what you want!'

Instantly, the building began to fill with cars and patio sets, ponies and computers and helicopters, microwave ovens, cuddly toys, speedboats, video-recorders and money. Amid the screams of delight which surrounded him, Dave heard the box in his pocket bleeping again and thought, with sinking heart, of Mr Purse.

He pushed his way between a conservatory and an ocean-going yacht to get to the lift. An electronic organ almost blocked his way at the last moment, but Dave managed to squeeze past it and slipped through the lift's open doors. He glanced at the row of buttons and pressed the top one which said, simply, PURSE.

The doors slid closed and the lift began to purr smoothly upward. Dave gazed at himself in its mirrored walls, still surprised by the sight of the grown-up man in a dark suit who gazed anxiously back. Somehow, he felt sorry for him. He straightened his tie.

Arriving on the top floor, Dave stepped out into the carpeted stillness of a vast room whose sloping glass roof showed the clouds scudding past outside. Behind them, the moon still hung in the sky, circular and blue.

At the far end of the room, an ancient, shrivelled man sat in a grey leather armchair. 'You are late,' he said. His voice was hardly more than a whisper, as dry as an autumn leaf which crumbles in the fingers. 'And you have lost your briefcase.'

For the first time, Dave realized that he had left the case behind at the police station. He had not seen it since the policemen who had arrested him had placed it on the table in front of the man with the shiny buttons. 'I couldn't help it,' he said. He wondered whether to wish the briefcase to reappear in his hand, and decided against it. Mr Purse would probably not like that sort of thing. 'I've been — busy,' he added lamely.

'So I see,' said Mr Purse in his dry whisper. 'Your progress has been most interesting.' With a slight movement of his head on its withered neck, he indicated a bank of television screens behind Dave, each one with a different picture on it.

Dave stared. He saw that the ground floor of the Megabiz building was crammed to the roof with stuff of all sorts, which kept changing as people found new and more extravagant things to wish for. On another screen, a tremendous clutter of cars was mixed up with trees and ducks and agitated policemen and people pushing prams and boys playing football. Next to it, Dave recognized the traffic warden, coming out of a travel agent's shop with two air tickets to Florida. In a restaurant window, a waiter was pasting up a notice which said, 'Customers must not consume their own food on these premises.' And Mr Sen, in a star-embroidered purple cloak, was doing something wonderful with white doves at a children's party.

Dave's smile faded as he saw on the neighbouring screen that two men in plain clothes were examining the contents of his briefcase. 'Oh, dear,' he said guiltily. 'I do hope those papers aren't anything important.'

'*Vitally* important,' whispered Mr Purse. 'They are the plan for our new, super-expensive luxury folly, which was scheduled for sale this Christmas.'

Dave's eyes had drifted back to Mr Sen, but he tore his attention away from the screen and gazed at Mr Purse instead. A luxury folly? What did he mean?

'A game,' went on Mr Purse, 'to be played on computers. But this was the game to end all games. The players could win articles of real value from each other. Money, of course, but also cars, houses, land. Everything. It would have been irresistible. We called it Gotcha.'

'Oh,' said Dave uneasily.

'The winners,' Mr Purse continued, 'get richer and richer. But the losers have to stop playing.' The corners of his mouth tightened a little in their folds and Dave realized that Mr Purse was smiling. 'They have nothing left to play with,' the dry voice went on with satisfaction. 'Not even their computers. The winners play each other, and again, those who lose drop out.'

'A bit like Musical Chairs,' Dave suggested, trying to lighten the oppressive atmosphere.

'Exactly,' Mr Purse agreed with satisfaction. 'In the end, there is just one winner left.'

'Then what?' asked Dave.

'Then,' whispered Mr Purse, leaning forward a fraction, 'that winner will play ourselves. Megabiz.'

Dave frowned. 'But what if you lose?' he objected.

Mr Purse put his finger-tips together and smiled again. 'My dear boy,' he murmured, 'you forget that Megabiz designed the game. We designed it, Dave, to win.' Dave watched the papery white hands as they parted and moved down to grip the grey leather of the chair's arms then, unwillingly, returned his gaze to the pale eyes. 'Yes,' said Mr Purse deliberately. 'With this game, we would have owned the world. And *you have left the plans in a police station.* What are you going to do about it?'

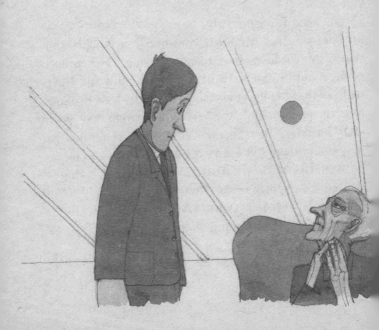

Dave's thoughts galloped with the desperation of a mouse in a wheel, getting nowhere. He could offer to wish the plans back but there was something even more frightening than the dry, ancient man who sat in front of him. The thought of Mr Purse owning the world was something which made Dave's mind flinch away. It made his joints feel weak and the palms of his hands clammy. It filled him with such utter helplessness that, grown up though he was, he wanted to cry.

Mr Purse was watching him. 'You could get them back, couldn't you, Dave,' he whispered. 'But it is too late for that. The men you see on the screen examining those papers are not fools. The secret is out. No, Dave. You will not get them back. But you will do something else.'

'What?' asked Dave, dry-mouthed.

'Sit down, boy — make yourself comfortable,' instructed Mr Purse, waving towards a grey-leather armchair like his own.

Reluctantly, Dave lowered himself into the chair, trying to sit upright on its edge, but its softness enveloped him and he lay back, feeling even more defenceless.

'You can make up for your unfortunate lapse, Dave,' whispered Mr Purse. 'You can make up for it beautifully.' He leaned forward suddenly. 'Give me your power to make wishes come true. If I have that, I do not need the game.'

45

'I don't think I ought to,' said Dave huskily.

Mr Purse uttered a croak of laughter. 'You should have thought of that before,' he said. 'Look what is happening downstairs.'

Dave turned his head to look again at the television screens. On the ground floor of the Megabiz building, fighting had broken out. The man who had asked Dave for a horse had evidently wished himself to be the commander of an army, for soldiers dressed in a simpler version of his own ornate uniform were charging with drawn swords at unarmed groups of people, trying to drive them out of the building. Within a few moments, an opposing army sprang up, commanded by a man standing by the nose of an executive jet. His soldiers were armed with rifles.

'Let us have a little volume,' said Mr Purse, getting up and crossing to a console of switches. The sound of screaming and crashing filled the room. Furniture was being smashed and people with cut and bleeding faces were punching each other. A close-up picture showed a squad of soldiers kneel down and level their rifles across a makeshift trench of up-ended washing machines, taking careful aim.

Dave twisted away. 'No!' he screamed. 'I WISH I'D NEVER GIVEN THEM ANYTHING!'

The crashing stopped. Nervously, Dave looked back at the screen and saw a man aim a last punch at another, but the room was empty of furniture and the soldiers had gone. There was no wreckage, and the people were unhurt. Looking puzzled, they began to drift back to their offices.

Mr Purse watched them. He seemed undisturbed by Dave's dramatic decision. He gave a faint shrug. 'You see what they are like,' he said. 'Winning would destroy them. Somebody has to be in charge. Somebody with complete power.' He approached Dave's armchair. 'You must not imagine that you yourself could fill such a role, Dave,' he said. 'Look what a mess you have made of this day. No. You must hand over the power.' He leaned over Dave, with his white knuckles pressing deep dents in the chair's grey leather arms. 'Give me the wish, Dave. Now.' The eyes in his wrinkled face were a pale, clear blue. The same blue, Dave thought in horror, as the moon. He put his hands over his face.

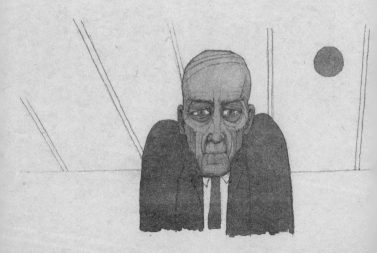

'I wish it had never happened!' he cried in bitter regret and had no thought in that moment that it was a request which might be granted. 'I wish I had never wished!'

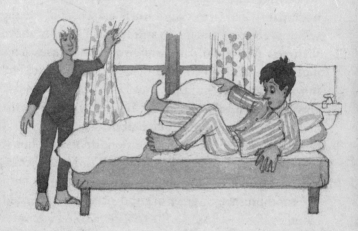

'Good morning,' said Primrose. 'It's a lovely day.' Dave sat up with a gasp of fright, and flung the bedclothes back to look at his feet. They were the usual size, and so were his arms and legs. His pyjamas fitted comfortably. He gave a sigh of relief and slumped back onto his pillows. 'Thank goodness for that,' he said.

'For what?' enquired Primrose.

'For it not being a blue moon day,' said Dave.

Primrose laughed. 'You've been dreaming,' she said. 'Do you want some breakfast? I'm just going to do my yoga.'

Dave sat up again, more slowly. *Had* it been a dream? Primrose was still looking at him enquiringly. 'I'd like some toast and peanut butter, please,' he said, 'if that's all right. I'll be down in a minute.'

When Primrose had gone downstairs, he pulled on his underpants and a tee shirt, then glanced out of the window to see if the moon still hung in the sky above the trees. And it did. Dave stared at it dubiously. This morning, the moon's round face looked as white and innocent as a saucer of milk, but Dave was not sure if it was to be trusted. He would have to try it out, he decided — but on something harmless.

He tiptoed across to the bedroom door and shut it quietly. He did not want Primrose to hear him. Then he returned to the window and looked out again. 'I wish my toothbrush was green instead of yellow,' he said aloud.

Nothing happened. His toothbrush still stood in the mug, a bright, clear, wonderfully permanent yellow. Dave looked at it and smiled. He pulled on his jeans and tied the laces of his trainers. The sense of relief made him feel as if he was walking on air. He opened the door and ran downstairs.

'We'll have breakfast in the garden,' said Primrose, who was strangely balanced on one foot. 'It's such a lovely morning.'

'*Isn't* it,' said Dave. Outside, he inspected the blue-flowered borage carefully. It seemed quite unsquashed — but then, he thought, he *had* wished it all right again as he drove the car out of the gate. The dream remained

51

oppressively real. He sat down in a faded deckchair. He could see Primrose's inverted feet through the kitchen window. It would probably be some time before breakfast arrived, he thought, but it didn't matter. Sue from Megabiz would not nag at him from the box in his jacket pocket. Mr Purse was not waiting.

Dave stretched luxuriously in his deckchair. Butterflies chased each other through the tall grass-heads and puffy white clouds moved across the sky. He felt extraordinarily happy.

After a while, Primrose came out with a tray and put it down on the garden table. 'Here we are,' she said. 'Pull up your chair.' As Dave did so, she added, 'There's a card or something sticking out of your pocket. Mind you don't lose it.'

Dave retrieved the card in some surprise and looked down to see what it was. Then the hair rose on the back of his neck and a shiver ran through his whole body. Printed in sloping, curly letters on the rather dog-eared card were the words, 'Mr Sen. Magician and conjuror. Children's parties a speciality.' And there was a London address and a telephone number.

Dave scrambled up from the deck chair and stood staring at the card. His face was flushed with excitement and dread. Was it all going to start happening again? 'Could I use the telephone?' he asked urgently. 'Please?'

'Yes, of course,' said Primrose, looking at him curiously. 'You know where it is, in the hall.'

Dave went into the house and dialled the number. Mr Sen had been such a nice man, and yet the thought of hearing his voice filled Dave with terror. After several clicks, the telephone gave out a continuous high-pitched buzz. Dave replaced the receiver and tried again, with the same result. He went slowly back to the garden and sat down.

'Toast?' offered Primrose.

'Thanks,' said Dave. He picked up the jar of peanut butter and paused with his hand on the lid. 'What does a continuous buzz mean?' he asked.

'Number unobtainable,' said Primrose. She reached for the card which lay beside Dave's plate and said, 'May I?'

Dave nodded.

Primrose read the card and said, 'No wonder you couldn't raise the number. There's a huge office block now where that little street used to be.'

'Megabiz,' said Dave with cold certainty.

Primrose laughed. 'That sort of thing, yes,' she agreed. 'What a wonderful name for it.' She glanced at the card again and looked faintly puzzled. 'Where did you get this?'

'I don't really know,' said Dave.

His grandmother sipped her camomile tea, then looked at him with concern. 'I hope you don't mind too much about being parked with me,' she said. 'It's probably the last time. You'll be grown up before you know it.'

The white moon hung like a ghost of itself in the blue sky. Dave smiled at his grandmother.

'There's no hurry,' he said.

The Deep Hole Day

One Saturday morning, Fergus began to dig a hole in the garden, down by the rhubarb, which had lots of feathery flowers and stems as thick as rolling-pins.

After a while, his mother, Babs, came out and watched. 'That's a very deep hole,' she observed.

'Yes,' said Fergus, and went on digging. 'It's going to be a pond.'

His mother clapped her hands in delight. 'With a little bridge over it, and coloured lights set in the banks!' she exclaimed. 'And a fountain! What a lovely idea!'

'I was thinking more of a boat,' said Fergus.

'Oh, don't be silly,' said Babs. 'A pond big enough to sail a boat on would have to be *huge*.'

Fergus did not reply. There was no point in having a pond unless it was huge. He went on digging, and Babs returned to the house, clasping a stick of rhubarb in both arms.

A little later, Hepworth came out, treading cautiously over the grass in his shiny black shoes. Hepworth was Fergus's father. He worked in an office and took things

seriously — especially the things he read in magazines. 'What's this about a pond?' he asked.

'Just an idea,' said Fergus. A couple of rhubarb stalks keeled over and fell into the hole.

'There are some very good bulldozers on the market,' Hepworth told him. 'It says in *Earthworks International* —'

'I'd rather just dig it,' said Fergus obstinately.

'Ah,' said Hepworth. 'Right.' He turned to survey the rest of the garden, hands in pockets. 'One of these days I shall landscape all this,' he said. 'A shrubbery over there by the coal bunker, then a sweep of lawn leading down to an arbour of roses. And a rock garden, starting somewhere near that old tricycle. And we could have giant carp in your pond.'

56

Fergus went on digging. He had noticed a long time ago that his father was not exactly a man of action, although he was brilliant about ideas on how to do things.

At lunchtime, Babs said, 'I really do think it's time we did something about the garden. I mean, apart from that awful rhubarb, it isn't a garden at all.'

'There's my pond,' Fergus pointed out, but his parents were not listening.

'It would cost thousands,' said Hepworth. 'This month's *Your Stately Home* puts the cost of grass seed alone at five hundred.'

'That was for a deer park,' said Babs.

Hepworth ignored her. 'Then there's terracing,' he went on, 'and planting and pergolas and topiary, not to mention carp. And peacocks fetch a pretty penny these days.'

'And coloured lights for the pool,' Babs agreed with a sigh.

'Coloured *lights*?' said Hepworth, frowning. 'That's unreasonable.'

Babs jammed the serving spoon back into the rather sour rhubarb crumble which nobody was enjoying very much. 'What do you mean, unreasonable?' she demanded.

'Waterproof bulkheads,' said Hepworth. 'Technically difficult. It says in *Sparks*, you should never —'

'Oh, *magazines*!' exclaimed Babs in disgust. 'I'm sick of magazines. When are you actually going to *do* something?'

Fergus held his breath. This was revolution.

Hepworth seemed dumbfounded. 'I go to work every morning!' he protested. 'I have done for years.'

'Yes, and we can't even afford a few little pond lights,' said Babs pathetically, shaking out a paper tissue as if it was a lace hanky. 'You were my hero, Heppy, when we got married. We had such dreams. And none of them have ever come true.' She gave a little sob.

'Oh, my dearest,' said Hepworth, pushing away his rhubarb crumble, 'have I failed you?'

'Yes,' said Babs.

Fergus listened in fascination, glad that neither of them seemed to mind that he hadn't eaten his rhubarb crumble.

'I shall look for a better job,' Hepworth promised. 'This month's *Dazzling Careers* is out today, so I'll have a good read through it this afternoon.'

Babs gave him a withering look and reached across to the sideboard for a copy of the *Wobbleswick Clarion*, which was folded back at the appropriate place. 'There's a job in the local paper,' she said. 'Look.'

' Startling prospects,' Hepworth read out reluctantly. ' Challenging post offering unexpected rewards for right person. Oh. Goodness.'

'If you've got nothing to do this afternoon, you could write to them,' said Babs.

'Er — yes,' said Hepworth, running a finger round the inside of his collar. 'I suppose I could.'

Fergus went back to his hole in the garden.

Days passed. The school holidays arrived, and Fergus had nothing to do except dig. Babs had lost interest in the pond since Hepworth had been so uncooperative about the coloured lights and in any case, she was busy with the Wobbleswick Ladies, doing Ethnic Arts. Fergus dug and dug, totally undermining the rhubarb and demolishing most of the grass. Gradually, the hole came to occupy the entire garden. Fergus dug a channel under the back fence, working his way towards the lake in the park, whose water he intended to borrow. It was all extremely interesting.

One evening, when Babs was at her Jazz and Joy class, the telephone rang. Fergus glanced up from his design for a boat as his father went to answer it.

'Hepworth Kidd speaking,' he said in his precise voice. 'Who?' His eyebrows shot up as he listened, and his frown was replaced by a polite smile. 'Maxamuse. Yes, indeed, I do remember you. I applied for a job with you some little time ago. . . . What, *now*?' He seemed startled. 'Isn't that somewhat unusual?. . . You're a very unusual firm. Yes, I see . . . oh, I am interested, yes, of course, but my wife's out, you see, and it's a question of who's to look after the boy . . . bring him along? Are you sure? . . . Yes, all right, straight away.' He replaced the receiver looking flustered.

'Bring him along where?' asked Fergus.

Hepworth was peering into the mirror anxiously, running a comb through his hair. 'To an interview,' he said, 'for a very important job. You will have to be extremely quiet and good.' He looked at his son with disapproval and added, 'Haven't you got a clean shirt?'

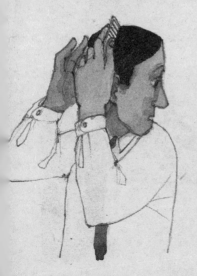

'I don't think so,' said Fergus. 'Mum used most of them for tie-dyeing and painting with melted candle-wax, only it didn't work.'

Hepworth sighed. 'Well, at least wash your face,' he said.

By the time Fergus came out of the bathroom after a dabble and wipe, Hepworth had managed to get the car started. He looked agitated. 'Hurry up, hurry *up*,' he said. 'Don't you realize this may be the chance of a lifetime?'

'Sorry,' said Fergus. He stared out of the car's window as they proceeded at a stately pace through the empty streets of the town in the dusty evening light. Hepworth refused to drive fast, even when he was in a hurry. He had read in *Prestige Limousines* that it was bad for cars to go quickly.

'What sort of place will it be?' asked Fergus.

'Maxamuse? Very large, I expect,' said Hepworth. 'With marble steps and a lot of glass. Ten-foot-high ferns and silently-gliding escalators. And secretaries called Amaryllis.'

Fergus nodded. He had glimpsed something like that in one of his father's magazines called *The Ultimate Office*. 'I'll watch out for it,' he said.

Hepworth found the right street and drove along it very slowly, looking from side to side. There were no buildings with marble steps or glass doors, but Fergus noticed a shop which sold silly hats and orange wigs, which seemed rather more fun. All the other shops in the street were small and dark, mostly selling Indian shirts and roast ducks and things made of brass. 'I think Mum would like it here,' he said.

Hepworth did not answer. He managed to park rather gracefully, because his was the only car in the street. He had never quite mastered the art of driving backwards, despite long hours of perusing *The Quintessential Chauffeur*. 'We shall have to reconnoitre on foot,' he announced, lapsing into *Survival For Scouts*.

'Okay,' said Fergus. He hopped out of the car and went to look in the window of the shop with the orange wigs, having a secret yearning for an artificial inkblot to deploy during Mr Pugh's maths lessons. Beside the shop was an open doorway, inside which a steep flight of brown-lino-covered stairs led upwards. When Hepworth came to join Fergus, he stood in this doorway, reading the cards on the wall. Then he cleared his throat in a slightly embarrassed way and said, 'It seems to be up here.'

Fergus detached his attention from the stink bombs and packets of itching powder and said, 'What is?'

'Maxamuse,' said Hepworth, pointing to one of the cards. 'Branch office, I expect.' He squared his shoulders and looked determined. 'Right,' he said. 'Over the top, chaps.'

War Stories For Boys, Fergus recognized, remembering the musty pile which his father had entrusted to him for safe-keeping when Babs was having a fit of tidying up.

Hepworth started up the stairs, marching very neatly in the centre of the worn treads, with his hands at his sides. Maxamuse was not on the first floor, nor on the second, nor the third. By the time they had toiled up yet another flight of stairs, Hepworth was leaning on the varnished handrail and wheezing like a kettle boiling dry.

'Here we are!' said Fergus cheerfully as they arrived on a small landing. The door in front of them had a frosted glass window in it on which was lettered the word, MAXAMUSE, in chipped black letters. A comfortable-looking chair stood invitingly beside it. 'Why don't you sit down for a minute?' Fergus suggested.

'Good idea,' gasped Hepworth. As he collapsed into it, the seat of the chair let out a long, loud, raucous raspberry which caused him to leap to his feet again.

'Come in!' sang a voice from behind the door, as if this was the normal way for visitors to introduce themselves.

Hepworth mopped his face with his neatly-folded hanky and straightened his tie again. Then he opened the door and he and Fergus both went in.

The room was small and hot, but all Fergus could see at first was a pair of enormous shoes with their soles towards him, the heels resting on a cluttered desk. On the left one, the word HOWDY was lettered in black paint, while the right one said, DOO? Fergus giggled.

The shoes lurched sideways to the floor, revealing their owner, a man in a flowered hat and a badly-darned navy sweater, sitting in a dilapidated office chair. His face was as crumpled and baggy-eyed as a bloodhound's. 'Name?' he enquired.

'Kidd,' said Hepworth, who was still very out of breath. 'Hepworth — Kidd.'

'Aha!' The man snatched off his flowered hat, revealing wispy red hair, and stood up to lean across the desk to shake Hepworth's hand. 'You're one of the maniacs who applied for the job. Great. We've had a couple of people started, but they didn't last. No stamina. I'm Phil O'Stein. Nothing too sacred for a joke, geddit?'

Hepworth looked pained. He glanced down at his hand, and Fergus saw that his father was holding a plastic fried egg, presumably transferred during the handshake. He tried not to giggle again, and the red-haired man winked at him. After a moment of indecision, Hepworth put the fried egg in his pocket.

Phil nodded. 'I like the straight face,' he said. 'Yes, you could have talent.' He turned his head slightly and shouted, 'Ammie! Come and look at this one!'

A section of the poster-plastered wall turned out to be a door, and through it came a girl wearing fishnet tights and feathers, with a spangle here and there. She put one hand on her hip and surveyed Hepworth thoughtfully, then nodded. 'He's got a very nice stuffed-shirt look, hasn't he,' she said. 'What's his name?'

'Hep Kidd,' said Phil. 'Hep, this is Ammie. My secretary.'

'Amaryllis Burne-Jones, actually,' said the girl as she shook hands with Hepworth.

'Oh, I say,' said Hepworth, impressed. This time, Fergus noticed, his father had been left holding a round, bright-red object, at which Phil nodded. 'Try it for size,' he instructed.

Experimentally, Hepworth pushed his finger into the red thing. Fergus nudged him. 'It's a clown's red nose,' he whispered.

'Oh,' said Hepworth. He put the red nose on, then quickly took it off again. 'What does this firm actually *do*?' he demanded. 'And what would my position be?'

Phil grinned. 'Your position would be thoroughly undignified most of the time,' he said. 'Maxamuse supplies entertainment, see. Send-ups, balloonograms, surprises, magic, kiddy-fun, practical jokes — call us and we'll lay it on.' He sat down in his dilapidated chair

and put his fingers together, gazing at Hepworth over the top of a grotesque pair of purple spectacles which had arrived on his nose. 'You will be aware, of course,' he intoned in a plummy voice, 'that the leisure industry is one of the country's leading growth areas.'

'Oh, yes, yes, quite,' agreed Hepworth, nodding enthusiastically. 'It said so in *Economics Simplified*.'

'There you are, then,' said Phil, and the spectacles leapt off his nose with a loud ping, hitting the ceiling and descending to the floor by means of a plastic parachute. 'We're a small firm, but the sky's the limit. I need a man who knows he's something special. A poet, a dreamer, an artist at heart — but able to take things as they come.'

'I am that man,' said Hepworth simply.

Phil looked at him with raised eyebrows. 'Of course,' he added, 'you may find some of the tasks a little below your dignity.'

'Try me,' challenged Hepworth, with his chin up like an illustration from *Heroism Through The Ages*.

'Okay,' said Phil.

There followed the most extraordinary ten minutes which Fergus had ever experienced. He watched with a kind of appalled hysteria while his father was embroiled in a series of unspeakable jokes. They involved umbrellas and feathers and water, exploding bouquets of paper roses, a chair which behaved like a jack-in-the-box and a flower which squirted red ink on the nose of anyone who smelled it. Hepworth was tripped up by the mat and by an umbrella handle, by Phil's shoe and by a stuffed dog. He utterly failed to balance a tin tray with glasses of lemonade on it on top of a chair leg, and somehow found himself jumping through a paper hoop while the stuffed dog didn't. He was showered with confetti and lemonade and torn paper flowers, soaked with water and crowned with strings of artificial sausages and finally bombarded with custard pies while trying in vain to retaliate as instructed. In fact, the only person he managed accidentally to hit was Fergus, who instantly grabbed a pie of his own and scored a bull's eye right in the middle of Phil's crumpled face.

'Good shot,' Phil said to him, blowing froth as he subsided into his office chair. 'We'll have you following in father's footsteps yet. Okay, Hep,' he added. 'You'll do. You're brilliantly uncoordinated. Got all the zippiness of a beached jellyfish. Start on Monday, right?'

Hepworth had collapsed on to a chair, regardless of the fact that it was playing a musical-box version of Brahms' Lullaby. He gazed up, red-nosed, dripping and panting, and said, 'No.'

'I thought he wouldn't,' said Ammie, retrieving a white rabbit from the wastepaper basket. 'You got it wrong, Phil. You want the sort who *knows* he's silly and doesn't mind. This one takes things seriously.'

'You may be right,' said Phil sadly.

Hepworth stood up, shedding wet confetti. 'I could not tell my wife,' he said with some dignity, 'that I had accepted a job as a custard-pie target. Come along, Fergus.'

On their way down the lino-covered stairs, they met a very fat man with yellow braces, labouring his way up. He gave them a perspiring grin. He looked just the man for the job, Fergus thought.

They drove home in silence. Somehow, Fergus liked his father better than he had ever done before. As they turned in at the gate, he said, 'I don't think you're silly.'

'Thank you,' said Hepworth. He switched the engine off and belatedly put the handbrake on as the car began to roll backwards out of the garage. Then he sat in silence for a few moments, picking moodily at the sodden paper rose petal which clung to his trousers. 'It sounded all right in the newspaper,' he said. 'And we all have our dreams.'

'Yes, we do,' said Fergus stoutly. He almost told his father about his own dream, of a pond big enough to sail a boat on, but decided to wait. Just a few more spadefuls, and he would reach the lake in the park to let the water in. 'Some dreams come true,' he said. 'You'll see.'

Babs gave a shriek of horror when Hepworth and Fergus went into the house. 'Heppy!' she screamed. 'Just look at your face! And your suit! What on earth has happened? Have you been mugged?'

'Taken for a mug,' said Hepworth gloomily, and told her all about it. When he got to the custard pies, Babs clapped her hands excitedly. 'So did you take the job?' she cried.

'No, of course not,' said Hepworth. 'You would have been ashamed of me.'

'Ashamed? Oh, Heppy.' She came and sat beside him on the sofa and twined her arms round his neck, careless

of his lemonade-soaked suit. 'I would have been proud
of you, darling. My hero. Such an unconventional job.'

Hepworth appeared to sag all over. 'Proud?' he
echoed weakly.

'Of course I would,' said Babs. 'I always dreamed of a
husband who was wonderfully mad and brave and
absurd. You talked about doing such amazing things,
Heppy, when we were first married, and I thought you
were really going to do them.'

Hepworth clasped his forehead in his hand, dislodging a pile of *You The Poet* from the arm of the sofa. 'My one chance,' he lamented, 'and I wrecked it.' He stared gloomily at the copies of *Self-Fulfilment* which lay on the floor, then transferred his gaze to Babs. 'I shall never read another magazine again,' he assured her. 'From now on, my dearest, I give you my word, it's practical action. I shall go into serious training as a stooge, so next time a job comes up I'll be in peak condition for it.'

Babs kissed him, getting pink dye all over her nose, and Hepworth wiped it off tenderly with his handkerchief and with Phil's plastic fried egg. 'We could set up in business on our own,' he said, inspired. 'Hep Kidd and Babs — Instant Fun.'

'Heppy, that's brilliant!' said Babs. 'I'll buy a pair of fishnet tights and some spangles tomorrow, as soon as the shops open. Darling, you're wonderful!'

Fergus tip-toed out and left them together.

Outside, the summer evening was still light enough to dig by. Fergus took his spade and attacked the last narrow piece of grass which stood between his pond and the lake in the park. This, he thought, was the day he would finish the deep hole. His mother and father deserved a nice surprise after their disappointment about the custard-pie job. He dug and dug. And, as the first star appeared in the sky, a trickle of water began to run from the lake in the park, down the channel he had dug, into the deep hole. He watched it with pride. Since the garden was slightly downhill from the park, the water ran readily, sweeping away loose stones and bits of earth. Fergus climbed back over the fence to see how his pond was getting on.

The muddy water was rising fast. A few withered rhubarb leaves floated on the surface, but it was beginning to look like a real, boat-sized pond. Through the French windows, Fergus could see his parents, deep in conversation.

Quite quickly, the deep hole filled up with water, which reached from fence to fence and swilled round the base of the coal bunker. Fergus went back into the park with his spade to stop the flow. Somewhat to his concern, he found that the channel he had dug was much wider and deeper now, scoured out by the torrent of water pouring into his pond. He dumped several spadefuls of earth into it to try and make a dam, but the gushing water washed his attempted blockage away with contempt.

Fergus felt panic sweep over him as he stared at the cascading water. He scrambled back into the garden and edged with difficulty past the brimming pond, which was now finding its way into the neighbouring gardens. He banged on the French windows, and saw his parents look up in surprise.

'Mum!' he shouted. 'Dad! I made a pond, but —'

Hepworth opened the French windows and stared out, gently shedding confetti. The water was lapping at his feet. His eyes bulged but he seemed unable to speak. Babs, looking over his shoulder, gave a strangled squawk. '*Fergus*!' she said. 'What have you *done*?'

80

'I borrowed the water from the lake,' Fergus explained. 'I only wanted a bit, but I've got all of it. You'll have to do something. I'm very sorry,' he added, as his parents stood aghast.

Babs recovered first, and rushed to the telephone. 'Fire brigade!' Fergus heard her shout. 'Quickly! With pumps!'

The water poured over the step and began to spread across the carpet.

'I really am sorry,' Fergus repeated wretchedly. 'It was meant to be a surprise.'

'Oh, it was,' Hepworth assured him as he and Fergus climbed on to the coffee table. 'But we all make mistakes. The trouble is,' he added thoughtfully, 'when dreams come true, they aren't dreams any more. Pity, really.'

The carpet had completely disappeared under the rising water, and the coffee table seemed likely to be engulfed at any moment.

'Perhaps we'd better get on the sideboard,' suggested Fergus.

Babs waded back from the telephone and said, 'They'll be here in a minute.' Fergus wondered why she didn't seem more upset. When Hepworth had helped her up to sit between him and Fergus on the sideboard, Babs said happily, 'Just think, we can probably claim on the insurance! For loss of furniture and carpets and rhubarb. Then we could start all over again and have things the way we really want them. We could even make a new garden. A proper one.'

'If we have to have a new floor,' said Hepworth tentatively, 'perhaps we could make it out of glass instead of wooden boards. And if Fergus put his pond underneath the house, we could sit and watch the carp swimming right below us. There was a converted water-mill like that in *Fabulous Homes*.'

'Wonderful!' said Babs enthusiastically. 'And we *can* have coloured lights, can't we?'

Hepworth smiled at her. 'Of course we can,' he said.

Fergus gave a sigh of relief. Everything was back to normal again. He began to think seriously about a design for a submarine.

The Sorting-Out Day

'One of these days,' said Phyllis as she gazed at the jam-packed jumble of a glory-hole which was Uncle Samuel's room, 'I'll sort this lot out.'

Ralph thought this was a good idea. 'Then I could have room of my own,' he agreed. 'I mean, it doesn't look as if he's coming back, does it — not after ten years.'

'Perhaps not,' his mother admitted. 'But then, the post could be very slow from the Upper Zambezi. I expect he's gone somewhere remote.'

'Trying out the Climbing Submarine,' said Ralph. He made a face as he glanced at the ceiling-high paraphernalia, and added, 'It looks as if he left half of it here. And I'm sick of sharing a room with Martin. He barks.'

'Toddlers do,' said Phyllis abstractedly. 'It's one of their stages. I keep thinking he'll write.'

'He's only two,' said Ralph.

His mother shook her head. 'Uncle Samuel,' she said. And that was the end of the conversation. Phyllis

85

wandered off downstairs to look for the tortoise in the garden, leaving Ralph to stare hopelessly at the roomful of stuff. He closed the door very gently, but even so, he heard a clatter from inside it as one of the smaller objects from the top of a teetering pile was dislodged by the slight shock. He gave a sigh as he watched his mother from the landing window, stooping among the delphiniums and holding her ribboned hat on with one hand as she called, 'Hannibal! Come along, darling — squashy plum time.' There was a basket at her feet, circled by hovering wasps.

Ralph sometimes despaired of his family. It was not that they were wilfully unhelpful, but they always seemed to be doing something else. With his father, it was the brass band. With Phyllis, it could be anything. This morning he had meant to ask her if she was coming to the school Sports Day. But he could imagine what the conversation would be like.

'How lovely!' Phyllis would cry. 'Strawberries on the lawn and people in white flannels.'

'Not really,' Ralph would tell her. 'Lines of chairs and Mrs Mountford with a starting gun.'

Phyllis would promise faithfully to be there, but on the day itself, somehow she would fail to arrive. Afterwards, she would look harassed and say, 'Fitting everything in is so difficult.' There would be some good excuse. 'I was up to the eyes in plum jam. All those stones. You didn't really mind, did you?'

And Ralph would say, with truth, 'Not really.'

Since Ralph did not run fast or throw anything very far, Sports Day for him consisted of a number of menial jobs such as pinning numbers on people's backs and retrieving javelins and raking the sand smooth in the jumping pit while the next competitor waited, shaking his or her hands and feet like a nervous horse. Ralph could see no reason why his mother should be present to watch him performing these tasks — but other people at school always seemed to fuss about her absence.

'Doesn't your mother come to *anything*?' Melinda

Marsh would say, gazing at Ralph soulfully from under her pale hair.

Ralph sighed again as he stared out across the garden and thought about Melinda. His mother had found Hannibal, and was smiling down at him as he slowly steam-rollered his way to and fro across the plums, in his usual pre-eating tenderising process. Melinda, Ralph thought, was amazingly nice, and she had huge blue eyes as well as all that fair hair; but her concern for his welfare made him feel hot with embarrassment. Being pitied was awful.

At school the next day, Melinda said, 'Is your mother coming to Sports Day?'

'No,' said Ralph.

'Oh, dear.' Melinda put her head sideways and looked sad.

Ralph scowled and said, 'She's busy.'

Melinda's head came upright. 'Is she?' she enquired with interest. 'What at?'

This was unexpected. After a moment's frantic thought, Ralph said, 'Erm — she invents things.' He blushed at the lie but, he thought, *somebody* in the family invented things — did it matter who?

'Really?' said Melinda, fascinated. 'Aren't you a dark horse — you never told me. What does she invent?'

Ralph's blush deepened. 'She's working on the Climbing Submarine,' he said, and, as Melinda continued to look expectant, 'it's designed to be self-powered over rough terrain, for exploring deep water in high places.'

'Like where?' asked Melinda.

'The Upper Zambezi,' said Ralph. 'Mostly.'

Melinda's blue eyes widened in respectful astonishment. 'Gosh!' she said.

The onset of a chemistry lesson saved Ralph from further questioning, but he knew Melinda would not leave it at that. He thought wildly as he heated something in a test tube over a Bunsen-burner flame. What else could his mother have invented? His brain-racking was interrupted by a small catastrophe as the end of the test-tube melted, showering the bench with its smoking contents. Miss Richards rushed up, scolding and mopping and Melinda beamed and said, 'Ralph's the absent-minded professor type — I expect he takes

after his mother. Did you know she's an inventor?'

Ralph closed his eyes in horror, but Miss Richards just said, 'Get on with your work, Melinda. Ralph Boggis, you are not fit to be entrusted with a pile of nursery bricks. Get a new test-tube from the rack, and *keep your mind on what you are doing.*'

'Yes, Miss,' said Ralph meekly. Climbing off his stool, he muttered to Melinda, 'Just you wait until they replace these old things with the Boggis burner. Contact-sensitized to prevent over-heating.'

'Fabulous,' said Melinda.

Naturally enough, the inventive genius of Ralph's mother was soon known to the entire form, and Ralph's own powers of invention were stretched to the uttermost as he strove to come up with a plausible-sounding series of contraptions to satisfy the endless questioning. Like tossing placatory sausage rolls to a wolf-pack, he offered them in quick succession the Automatic Plum-Stoner, the Thermostatically-Controlled Tortoise Hibernator, and a bedtime cassette tape for toddlers called Bow-wow To You, Too, recorded entirely by dogs. They gobbled up these tidbits and demanded more.

'I'll have to check with Mum,' Ralph said desperately. 'A lot of it is still on the secret list, you see.' They nodded, looking as if they quite understood, but Ralph knew the respite was only temporary.

Thank heavens, he thought, the weekend lay ahead. There would be time to dream up some more ideas.

Saturday and Sunday did indeed provide some useful nuggets of invention. The Motor-Powered Wheely-Basket popped into Ralph's mind as he helped his mother lug the shopping home from the supermarket. That afternoon, as his father trudged perspiringly to and fro across the grass with the lawnmower, Ralph made a mental note about Self-Limiting Dwarf Grass Seed, guaranteed not to grow more than half an inch tall. Tea-time, with Martin in his highchair, supplied an obvious need for Bouncing Buns, which picked themselves up each time they were hurled to the floor, and bath-time suggested the Splash-Proof Wash Capsule, thus saving an awful lot of mopping-up.

On Sunday morning, Ralph's father, Leonard, came back from conducting the band concert in the park, muttering darkly about absenteeism among irresponsible players who chose to catch pneumonia or go on honeymoon, and Ralph gave a little hiccup of excitement as the notion of the Cortromba sprang, ready-made, into his mind. This would be a single instrument capable of combining the highest cornet notes with all the trombone noises, ranging down to the deepest grumbles of the tuba. He thought about it seriously while practising his euphonium, and, afterwards, did

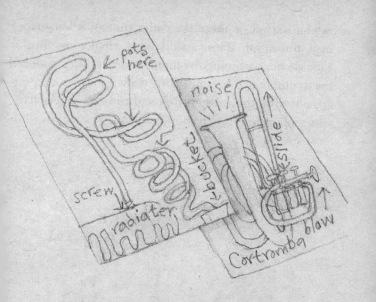

some working drawings of the revolutionary new instrument. He was rather pleased with them.

The Cortromba principle also gave Ralph the Unipipe Multipot which could cook an entire meal, using a single serpentine pipe which coiled round all the saucepans. You simply connected it to any handy radiator. That evening, Ralph made some further drawings of all his inventions, together with copious notes, then crawled into bed, exhausted. Untroubled by Martin, who was, as usual, yapping gently in his dreams, he fell asleep.

The hard-won yield of the weekend was devoured in a few minutes by Ralph's classmates, then a large, solid boy called Bert Hogg wanted to know why Ralph's mum didn't invent 'something good'.

Ralph looked at him warily and asked, 'What exactly had you in mind?'

Bert shrugged. 'All this stuff what you been talking about,' he said. 'It's all small stuff, innit? Like, household goods. Kind of thing you buy in Woolworfs.'

'I hardly think that you could buy the Climbing Submarine in Woolworths,' said Ralph icily.

'Yeah, but who wants one of them?' said Bert. 'In any case you could make one easy enough. All you'd want is an old rotavator and a plastic sack.'

Ralph felt himself sag at the knees as he gazed at Bert's pink, obstinate face, but Melinda came to his rescue. 'That just shows how stupid you are, Bert Hogg,' she said with contempt. 'You have to build prototypes and all that, don't you, Ralph?'

'Prototypes,' said Ralph weakly, wondering why he hadn't thought of the word himself. 'Oh, yes. We've got a whole roomful of those.'

'There you are, then,' said Melinda triumphantly. 'So you can go and boil your head, Bert.'

Ralph toyed with the idea of the Steam-Powered Leak-Proof Head-Boiler, but quickly dismissed it, and the bell went for Maths.

Doodling absently as Mr Webber rambled on about the geometry of circles, Ralph brooded over Bert's criticism. There was a grain of truth in what he had said. Domestic inventions were all very well, but they lacked drama. There was no real thrill about the Bouncing Bun. Thrills, spills, danger. . . . Ralph nibbled the end of his pencil as he gazed at the back of Bert's crew-cut head. Bert liked computer games, motor-bikes, fairground rides — Mr Webber paused for a moment in what he was saying as Ralph Boggis gave a stifled yelp of inspiration and began to work in a sudden frenzy of interest. The master took off his glasses and polished them in self-congratulation. It was not often that one achieved such a break-through.

After a couple more days' work during every lesson except Singing and P.E., Ralph had completed the preliminary designs for the Personal Death-Ride Simulator, a spring-mounted man-sized globe whose interior consisted of a three-dimensional television screen, giving the occupant the illusion of a complete roller-coaster track. Powered by a modified motor-cycle engine, the capsule could be hurtled about within its framework, tilted and swung and dropped and generally guaranteed to make the occupant emerge queasy and shaking with exhilaration.

Bert was impressed. 'That's more like it,' he admitted as he riffled through the drawings during Miss Witty's French conversation lesson. 'I wouldn't mind having one of them. What's it going to cost?'

'Difficult to say,' said Ralph loftily. 'That sort of thing isn't really Mum's department.'

Bert nodded sagely and said, 'They'll do all that in Accounts.'

'Quite,' said Ralph.

Time passed, and Ralph began to regret the Personal Death-Ride Simulator as Bert enquired daily as to its progress. He took refuge in pleading that it was still in the development stage, or that other small projects had cropped up, but Bert Hogg was insatiable, and Melinda's protective smile grew troubled.

'You know,' she said to Ralph one day, 'it must be awful, living with a mother who's so clever. It makes you feel so inferior, doesn't it, trying to understand what she's up to. I'm really sorry for you.'

Once again, Ralph sagged. He just couldn't win.

At home, too, his preoccupation was noticed. 'You're looking pale, boy,' his father said kindly. 'More deep breathing is what you need. You can come along to band practice. You're good enough now — and we could do with another euphonium player. One of ours is going to have a baby just before the Town Hall concert. Pretty inconsiderate of her.'

Ralph joined the band and played in the Sunday morning concerts in the park, wearing a slightly over-large uniform — but he remained anxious.

As his birthday approached, Phyllis announced, 'This year, you can have a really lovely party, and ask everyone in your form. The band can play in the garden and we'll shut Hannibal in the tool-shed and have a bonfire, with baked potatoes and sausages.'

Ralph turned even paler, but said bravely, 'Thank you very much.' There was a good chance, he thought, that his mother would forget about it or decide to do something else. The prospect of his whole class coming to the house, where it would be perfectly obvious that his mother had never invented anything in her life, was devastating. He thought of Bert Hogg's sarcasm. He could not even contemplate Melinda's wordless reproach.

But Phyllis did not forget about the party. As the day approached, she got out a step-ladder and began to hang lights in the trees. In the evenings, she made wonderfully elaborate paper hats, and wrapped up a lot of mysterious small parcels for the bran tub, which was a huge packing-case she had extricated from Uncle Samuel's room and covered with red-and-white paper. She gave Ralph several packets of invitation cards with pictures of crossed champagne glasses in the corner, and a pen

which wrote in gold. 'There you are,' she said. 'Ask everyone you like. If you need more cards, just say.'

Ralph gulped. 'Thanks ever so much,' he said, and gave his mother a kiss and a hug. He could not explain that the thought of the party filled him with dread.

The invitations were accepted with alacrity. Everyone wanted to come and meet Ralph's amazing mother and, even more, to see the inventions. On several occasions, Ralph tried hard to bring himself to tell them that his mother wasn't an inventor at all — but somehow, his courage failed him each time. His classmates would be so cross when they found out he had been having them on. Probably none of them would come to the party at all, and then his mother's wonderful preparations would be wasted and she would be dreadfully upset. Ralph went about with his fingers secretly crossed, and prayed for a miracle.

Leonard composed a piece called Birthday Cakewalk, which was supposed to be a big surprise, except that he kept rehearsing the flugelhorn part in the tool-shed in the evenings, and the tune drifted up to where Ralph lay in bed and worried.

'Birthday song,' said Martin, and growled. 'Not tell you. Secret.' The house was full of delicious baking smells and on the morning of the party itself, a Saturday, Phyllis was up at dawn, in a frenzy of whipped cream and pink sugar strands.

103

'You seem to be very early with everything,' said Ralph as he gazed, appalled, at the array of trifles and meringues and iced fancies with cherries on top. There was no doubt about it — this party really was going to happen.

Phyllis looked smug. 'I have been amazingly efficient,' she said.

'*I* haven't,' Leonard admitted. 'But there's plenty of time. I thought you might like to choose a birthday present, then we'd have lunch somewhere and take a boat down the river, keep out of your mother's hair.'

'Great,' said Ralph.

The day passed in a dream. He became the owner of several brass-band tapes and a large, heavy book called *Eccentric Inventions of the Victorian Age* which might, he thought, come in handy if he managed somehow to get through the party with his credibility intact. Trailing his fingers in the water as Leonard rowed down the river, Ralph made a decision. He would confess everything to his mother, and beg her to pretend she was an inventor. She would not be good at it, for Phyllis never pretended about anything, but it was the only hope. He looked at his father and smiled. Leonard was pom-pomming happily to the Sousa march playing in his personal stereo and rowing in strict tempo. Ralph put on his own headphones and furtively slipped in a Queen cassette. Then he leaned back against the boat's transom and gazed up at the cotton-wool clouds marching past in their blue sky. With faint surprise, he found that he was enjoying his birthday immensely.

They were a little late in returning, as Leonard had become engrossed in Pomp and Circumstance and forgot about the time. Cars were already parked outside the gate, and the band could be heard warming up in the back garden. Leonard and Ralph walked down the path which led round the side of the house. Then they stopped dead.

'Heavens!' said Leonard faintly.

The lawn was covered with the contents of Uncle Samuel's room. Every gimcrack, preposterous contraption which had ever been stored cheek by jowl with its outlandish neighbour now stood or lay on the grass

between the white-clothed tables and the crates of lemonade. The newly-arrived guests were inspecting them gingerly, and Bert Hogg was saying something disparaging. Martin was sitting in a wooden object with fins and wheels and part of an engine, thumping an imaginary horn and shouting, 'Brrm! Brrm!' It made a change from barking, Ralph thought.

The band, loosely grouped among plywood propellers and things made of riveted aluminium, gave a ragged cheer as they saw Ralph, and a rash young cornet-player tootled the opening phrase of the Birthday Cakewalk.

'*Shush*!' bellowed Leonard, hastening towards them across the grass. 'Wait for *me*!' He seized his baton and glared round at the band, arms upraised. 'Right! Now — after four.'

The familiar tune rang in Ralph's ears as he rushed in through the back door and charged up the stairs to Uncle Samuel's room, amid an increasing smell of new paint. His mother turned to smile at him, brush in hand, as he stood panting in the doorway. 'I finished the party stuff so early,' she said, 'I thought I'd do something else. Surprise for you.'

Ralph stared round at the fresh, primrose-yellow walls. His bed already stood in the middle of the otherwise empty floor. 'It's wonderful,' he said. 'But — I thought you were waiting for Uncle Samuel to write.'

'He did,' said Phyllis. 'There was a card in the post this morning, just after you went out. "Decided to stay," it said. "Redesigned submarine as Nutgatherer. Very intelligent people here. Raining. Love, Sam".'

'When was it posted?' asked Ralph.

'Four years ago,' said Phyllis.

Ralph nodded. 'What are we going to do with all that stuff outside?' he asked.

'I've no idea,' said Phyllis, 'but it's not coming back in here. Did you like the Cakewalk?' she added as the music in the garden came to an end.

'Yes,' said Ralph, and felt dreadful about not being out there. He grabbed his euphonium from the landing and ran down the stairs again, and out of the back door to the garden where, a little breathlessly, he played the solo he had been practising. It was called, Thank You Very Much.

When it was over, and he had shaken his father's hand in congratulations on the new composition, and been thumped on the back by a couple of hefty trombonists, Ralph suddenly remembered that he had not asked Phyllis about pretending to be an inventor. He turned to go back to the house — and found Melinda standing beside him.

'Happy Birthday,' she said. 'Here's your present.'

It was a chemistry set, with a card saying, 'To Professor Boggis, with love.'

'Thanks,' said Ralph. 'It's terrific.'

'I think it's a bit silly,' said Melinda. 'My mother got it. You know how parents do. I suppose it was because I told her about you melting the test-tube.'

Ralph nodded. That had been right back at the beginning of it all. He glanced up at the window of Uncle Samuel's room. There was still time to see Phyllis. 'I'll be back in a second,' he said. 'I've just got to —'

But at that moment, his mother came out of the back door and crossed the lawn towards him, with a jelly in one hand and a paint brush in the other. 'I want lots of people to come and help carry the food into the garden,' she announced.

Everyone rushed towards the kitchen except Bert Hogg, who stayed where he was, moodily kicking at a cluster of strangely-shaped tanks. He looked up at Phyllis, scowling, and said, 'I thought you were supposed to be an inventor.'

Ralph closed his eyes. The band's rendering of Spread A Little Happiness hammered in his brain.

'Oh, no, not me,' he heard his mother say. 'I just invent things like parties.'

'Ralph said you invented all this stuff,' Bert persisted. 'But none of it works.'

'Useless,' Phyllis agreed. 'It's a load of rubbish.'

'Right,' said Bert. He sounded puzzled. 'Whose is it, then?'

'It *was* Uncle Samuel's,' said Phyllis, 'but he won't be wanting it any more.'

Bert gave Ralph an accusing stare and Ralph looked away, just as Martin collided with his knees, driving an imaginary car. 'Brrm, brrm!' Martin said fiercely, turning his steering-wheel from side to side. 'Hoo-oot!'

For once, Ralph was rather glad to see his little brother. He bent down, hiding his blushing face as he deflected Martin on to a fresh course. 'Drive over there,' he instructed. From above him, he heard an odd snorting noise. He risked a glance upwards to see that Melinda had a hand pressed to her mouth as she glanced from Bert to Ralph and tried to restrain her giggles. Phyllis was looking perplexed and Bert, with his hands in his pockets, had turned to frown thoughtfully at the piles of junk.

There was something very infectious about Melinda's amusement. Ralph grinned guiltily — and suddenly felt much better about the whole thing.

Bert glanced over his shoulder at Ralph's mother and said, 'My dad might buy this lot off you.'

'Really?' Phyllis cocked her head with polite interest. 'Is he an inventor, too?'

'No,' said Bert. 'He's a scrap man.'

Melinda collapsed into fits of laughter.

'Don't see what's funny,' said Bert. 'He'll give you a fair price.'

Phyllis, too, began to laugh. 'Poor Uncle Samuel,' she said, wiping her eyes with the back of the hand which held the brush. 'He thought they were such wonderful inventions.' Ralph noticed that she had left a smudge of yellow paint on her hair.

'Who *is* Uncle Samuel?' asked Melinda.

Ralph took a deep breath. 'He's the one who invented all this stuff,' he said. 'I don't know why I said it was Mum. Silly, really.'

'You invented an inventor!' gurgled Melinda. 'What a hoot! You are wonderful, Ralphie.' And she took his hand and squeezed it.

Bert was gazing at Ralph in astonishment. 'Did you make up all them things, then?' he asked. 'The Personal Death-Ride Simulator and all that?'

'Yes,' admitted Ralph. 'I'm awfully sorry.'

'Blooming brilliant,' said Bert.

All around them, party food was piling up on the tables. The band, eyeing it, galloped through Getting To Know You, then put their instruments down and approached hungrily.

'The sausages!' cried Phyllis. 'I meant to cook them over the bonfire but I forgot all about it.'

'Could knock you up a nice little barbecue out of some of this stuff,' offered Bert, indicating the junk.

'I'll help you,' said Ralph.

'Me, too,' said Melinda.

'Lovely,' said Phyllis.

That night, lying in bed in his new room, Ralph smiled.
The party had been a huge success, and nobody seemed
to mind a bit about his invented inventor. The sound of
Martin hooting impatiently in his sleep drifted faintly
through the wall and Ralph felt doubly glad to have a
room of his own. The car stage, he thought, might be
even noisier than the dogs.

Moonlight shone through the curtainless windows, making pale shapes across the primrose-yellow walls. Apart from Ralph's bed, which still stood in the middle of the floor, the room was empty. Ralph gazed at it with pleasure. It was going to be so useful to have all that space. Tomorrow, he thought, before Bert's father arrived to shift the junk, he would get up early and retrieve a few of the more useful bits and pieces. Bert was quite right. The Personal Death-Ride Simulator was a good idea, there was no doubt about that. And now he had a room of his own, he could build a prototype.

Ralph yawned. All he would need was a secondhand motor-bike and a very big globe-shaped tank and several old television sets. Oh, and a computer, of course, and quite a lot of steel scaffolding and some springs — and nuts and bolts . . . and a hacksaw . . . and a hammer. . . .

Smiling again at the thought of the wonderful inventions which lay ahead, he fell blissfully asleep.

The Two-Day

'You could take some of Auntie's clothes to school tomorrow,' said Julia's mother at tea-time. 'They're too good to put in a jumble sale. I'm sure your Drama teacher would appreciate them for the Wardrobe.'

'We don't really have a Drama teacher,' said Julia. 'There's Miss Palethorpe, but she's just English. And anyway, we're going to the Botanic Gardens tomorrow, to aid our powers of description.' Auntie's clothes were horrible, she thought. They smelt of moth-balls.

'You'll be going to school as normal before you get on the bus,' said her mother. 'You can take a bag with you. It's a lot of work, sorting out a house after someone's died.'

'Yes,' said Julia meekly, but hating the idea of Auntie's old clothes. Everyone would giggle. They tended to giggle at Julia, at the best of times.

'Are you awake?' her mother called up the stairs the next morning. 'Yes,' said Julia sleepily.

'You'll want to leave in good time,' went on her mother, 'if you're going to take that bag of clothes in.'

Julia groaned. It would be very nice to sink back into

sleep again, she thought, and not have to face this day at all. She hoped the bag of clothes would not be a very big one.

But it was. Between mouthfuls of toast and absent-minded sips of tea, Julia's mother kept popping out to the front room where Auntie's things had been stacked. Julia could hear openings and shuttings of suitcases, and when her mother at last came into the kitchen and said, 'Here we are, then,' the bag she was lugging was enormous — a black, shiny, plastic bin bag, bulging hugely.

'Oh, *no*,' protested Julia.

Her mother looked reproachful. 'I thought you were a *helpful* girl,' she said.

Julia sighed. People were always saying that kind of thing. She looked at the clock. Heavens! She was going to be late. How appalling! Julia had never been late for school, ever.

The bag was so big that it made her feel quite unbalanced as she struggled up the High Street with it, past the Bingo Hall and round the corner into the narrower roads which led to the school. It was a windy day, and the breeze caught the bag like the sail on a boat, causing Julia to zig-zag drunkenly along the pavement. *Way-hay and up she rises*, she sang to herself, amused in spite of her panic about being late. How would Miss Palethorpe cope with a drunken sailor in her class?

A little gang of dogs came bouncing out of an alleyway and barked at the bag and in backing away from them, Julia collided with a railing and felt one of its spikes catch at the plastic and tear it.

'Oh, *no*,' she said again, and lowered the bag to the ground to see what damage had been done. A piece of fur was sticking out of the tear, and she had a brief argument with a fox terrier about ownership of it, then heaved the bag into both arms and staggered on, clutching it like a vast baby and unable to see where she was going.

After several misadventures with lamp-posts and some cautious feeling her way down pavement edges and across roads, Julia at last arrived at the school gates, only to see the bus already coming down the drive, with the girls in her form staring at her through its windows and squealing with laughter. The bus stopped and its door hissed open, and Miss Palethorpe said, 'Julia, what on *earth* have you got there? Come along, quickly. It's not like you to be late.'

Julia sat down on the only remaining empty seat, lugging the bag on to it beside her.

'Julia's a *good* girl,' said Rhona Cheeseman from behind her. 'Julia's *never* late. What have you got in the bag, Julia — packed lunch?'

Everyone giggled again, and Julia tried to smile. She sometimes dreamed in wilder moments that Rhona Cheeseman was her friend. Rhona had long legs and chewed gum and wore her school uniform with subtle differences which made her look somehow inspirational. She made Julia feel dull. Sitting beside the black plastic bag, Julia gave a small sigh. Yes, she thought that was the trouble. She was dull.

When the bus arrived at the Botanic Gardens, Miss Palethorpe stood up and said, 'I do not want anyone to imagine that this is merely a *jaunt*. As I have told you, each part of these gardens has a distinct and beautiful atmosphere, and I would like you to extend your spiritual antennae, as if you were hyper-sensitive insects. Notice everything, and assign to it the appropriate adjective.'

Rhona smothered a tiny yawn, and Miss Palethorpe looked down her nose at her. 'Enter into the *spirit* of the thing,' she added with a trace of exasperation. 'Now, when we leave the bus, will you please walk in twos, at least as far as the Cold House.'

And then in freeze, Julia thought idiotically. The other girls poured down the gangway of the bus to the door as she sat marooned beside the bulky bin bag. When they had all gone out, she got up and began to squeeze past it.

A young man bounded up the steps of the bus and said, 'Ah! You're the girl with the fancy dress. Wonderful!'

Julia gazed at him doubtfully. He had a curly red beard and wore a waistcoat over a grubby but theatrically full-sleeved white shirt. His trousers were tucked into cuffed boots. He looked, she thought, as if he was pretending to be Robin Hood. 'Fancy dress?' she queried, and felt duller than ever.

'The bag!' explained the young man, waving his hand at it. 'Just what we need!' He swung it to his shoulder and the escaping fur dangled behind him like a tail as he turned on the steps of the bus to offer Julia a courtly hand. 'I am your guide to the Gardens,' he told her.

The crocodile of girls, with Miss Palethorpe at its head, waited impatiently for Julia. The last pair, Letitia Willowes and Margot Plum, regarded her reproachfully as she took up her place behind them. 'You haven't got a two,' said Margot unkindly. 'No,' agreed Julia. Somehow, on occasions like this, she very seldom had.

'I'll be your two,' said the young man, and fell into step beside her as they followed the line of girls through the high wrought-iron gates into the Gardens. It was odd, Julia thought, that nobody turned to giggle at the sight of her walking in the company of a male person, let alone someone who looked like Robin Hood. Perhaps Miss Palethorpe had introduced him to the girls while Julia was still in the bus, and delivered one of those warning stares through her gold-rimmed glasses.

As they walked between the neat beds of geraniums and past the floral clock, Julia gave some serious thought to the problem of being dull. Perhaps she had been doing things all wrong, she mused. 'Be good, sweet maid,' her mother was fond of saying, 'and let who will be clever.' Rhona Cheeseman had it the other way round. Perhaps, Julia thought, it was all a question of being brave enough to speak to people before they spoke to you. She stole a glance at the red-bearded young man who paced amiably at her side with the bin bag over his shoulder and sought desperately for a topic of conversation.

'Do you take all the school parties round the Gardens?' she ventured.

'No,' he said. 'I'm just here for you.'

'Oh,' said Julia. It was an unhelpful response, baffling and somehow personal. After a pause, she said, 'My name's Julia Murgatroyd.'

'People call me all sorts of things,' said the young man. 'Mostly just Mr E.'

'Like, E for elephant?' suggested Julia.

'E for anything,' said the young man. 'You can call me Gene if you like.'

It sounded like a girl's name, Julia thought. Politely, she said, 'Is it American? There was a dancer called Gene Kelly. I've seen him in old films. He's wonderful.'

'Isn't he just!' the young man agreed. 'I love dancing, don't you?'

Julia thought of the school's Christmas disco, when the boys from St Dominic's had been invited. She had sat on a gym bench by the wall in her best dress, holding a glass of Coke which got warmer and stickier as the evening went on and watching the circling the coloured lights made across walls and ceiling, until their repeated circling began to seem tired and sad. 'I don't think I'm very good at it,' she said.

'Yes, you are,' said Gene firmly. 'You'll see.'

The crocodile came to a halt outside the Cold House. 'In here,' Miss Palethorpe was saying, 'you will find evidence of life's tenacity against all odds. Ebullient.

130

Triumphant. Think of hurtling across the frozen
steppes in a troika, with bells jingling on the harness.'

Rhona Cheeseman muttered something about her uncle Arthur slipping on the frozen steps and spending three months in hospital, but Miss Palethorpe ignored her and ushered everyone in through the heavy, white-painted metal door.

The Cold House was warmer than Julia had expected, due to the sun which kept glinting from behind the scudding clouds outside, but it was decidedly bleak. Small grey plants grew among outcrops of rock, and there was a group of lugubrious pine trees in the corner. Gene put the bin bag down and dug about in it, hauling out the fur which Julia had rescued from the fox terrier. It turned out to be part of a large, soft, furry hat. Then he produced a dress with a wide leather belt, and high heeled boots.

'Put them on,' he instructed. 'Over there behind the rocks. No-one'll notice.'

Julia stared at him, astounded.

'I'm going to see about the music,' said Gene, making for the door.

'But did Miss Palethorpe —'

'She'll love it,' said Gene. 'Atmosphere. Back in a minute.' And he had disappeared outside.

Julia hesitated, clutching the armful of clothes. The girls were clustered round Miss Palethorpe, who was saying something poetic about an edelweiss. None of them were looking in Julia's direction. She retreated behind the rocks and inspected the dress. It was made of warm red wool with a cross-stitched pattern round the hem. Impetuously, she took off her blazer and pulled the dress over her head, buckling the belt tightly. She wriggled out of her school skirt, then tugged on the high-heeled boots. With the furry hat pulled down over her eyebrows, she thought, nobody would recognize her.

Gene came back through the door, herding before him a trio of sulky-looking men in embroidered blouses, carrying balalaikas. They sat down on the edge of the stones labelled Arctic Scree and burst into a wild *czardas*. Julia emerged nervously from behind the rocks and Gene took her hand and smiled at her.

'*Now*!' he shouted — and in the next instant, she found herself swept into the dance.

With so much stamping and kicking going on, there was no time to be embarrassed — and besides, Julia felt an intoxicating glow of virtue in obeying Miss Palethorpe's instructions so exactly. She had, in very truth, entered into the spirit of the thing.

'Bravo!' said Gene as the music ended. Blushing, Julia was aware of applause. Miss Palethorpe was looking amazed. Julia dived for the shelter of the rocks.

Gene was waiting for her when she came out of the Cold House. The others, she saw, had moved on to a much larger glass building whose transparent roof revealed a forest of lush greenery within it. 'The Tropical House,' said Gene, nodding at it. 'Boiling hot in there, so we'll do something languorous. A tango, I think. Frightfully decadent. You can change behind the mangroves.' Relieving Julia of the Russian outfit, he thrust a new bundle of clothes into her arms.

This time, she found a mushroom-coloured tea-gown embroidered with strange brown roses, together with thin-strapped cream shoes and a feather for her hair. The girls, she saw as she scuttled to the seclusion of the tall, dripping plants, were already seated expectantly by the lily pool, while an old-fashioned gramophone with a curving gilt horn played a plaintively passionate tune. Under the palm trees and the dangling creepers, she danced with growing abandon, and Gene held a red rose between his teeth and did not seem to mind the slow drips of water which fell on them from the glass roof,

136

high above the banana trees.

This time the applause was even more enthusiastic. 'Astonishing,' said Miss Palethorpe, with hibiscus petals in her hair, and her glasses misting in the tropical heat. 'Such empathy.' Rhona Cheeseman chewed in moody jealousy.

In the Elizabethan Garden, Julia trod a stately measure between the clipped box hedges, wearing a dress with a tight bodice, and a velvet cap embroidered with pearls. The musicians, sitting in an arbour of honeysuckle, played flutes and viols, and the scents of thyme and rosemary, lavender and catnip sweetened the air of the morning. The girls minuetted on the camomile lawn, to Miss Palethorpe's delight, and the last of the clouds blew away to reveal a beaming sun.

The musicians finished their piece and stood up, sweeping off their hats in a bow, and Julia, with her hand in Gene's, curtsied deeply.

'Good old Jools!' said Margot Plum, thumping Julia on the back. 'What a hoot!' Then she rushed after the others, in the direction of the Cactus House.

'Wonderful, dear,' said Miss Palethorpe. 'Quite inspirational.'

Julia, unpinning her velvet cap behind a grove of damask roses, felt a surge of happiness. Not only was she entering into the spirit of the thing, but she was managing not to be dull, as well. Folding up the long dress with its stiff lace collar, she went skipping out to meet Gene. 'What next?' she enquired.

'A touch of the Old Nile,' said Gene. He glanced at the baggy sleeves of his shirt and added, 'Perhaps I'd better take this off. It doesn't seem very Eastern.'

'You want baggy trousers and a turban,' said Julia.

'Turbans are easy,' said Gene, 'but we're short on baggy trousers. I did spot a pair of jodhpurs, though.'

'They'll do,' said Julia. 'You can be an explorer, instead.'

The Cactus House was even hotter than the Tropical House, though dry and sandy, and the girls were fanning themselves with the clip-boards on which they were supposed to be taking notes, and gasping. The musicians had removed most of their clothes (though they had managed to improvise turbans), and sat cross-legged on the floor, playing sinuous tunes on long pipes.

Julia slipped behind a giant mammalaria, where she wriggled into some jewelled undies and a lot of veils, keeping a cautious eye on the prickles. There was no trace of moth-balls about the clothes, she noticed; they had, in fact, a faint, enticing hint of spiciness. There must have been more to Auntie than met the eye. To renewed applause, she glided out to meet Gene, who had found a solar topee and a somewhat over-large safari jacket as well as the jodhpurs. Together, they wove a pattern of such graceful movement that Letitia Willowes said she felt quite faint, though Rhona told her cattily to stop trying to get into the act.

'Just one more experience, girls,' Miss Palethorpe called, clapping her hands as her charges streamed across the grass towards the Orangery, 'then we will have to rejoin the bus. Miss Bing needs it for lacrosse.'

Following with Gene, Julia eyed the graciously-arched building whose tall glass doors stood open to the terrace and said, 'What do we do here?'

'Audience participation,' said Gene. 'I've alerted a few of the gardeners, to add a bit of masculine charm. They're bringing their own glad-rags. We'll have, as they say, a ball.'

In the shadowed hollow of opulently-blooming rhododendrons, Julia made her last change, into elbow-length lacy gloves, satin slippers and an Empire gown with layer upon layer of floating tulle and a rose at the bosom. Wrapped in the middle of the bundle of clothes, she found a little ivory fan, each blade intricately patterned with delicate fretwork.

Gene was waiting for her on the velvety lawn, attired in immaculate evening dress, complete with a long cape lined with scarlet silk. Julia gasped at the sight of such beauty and then, with her hand on his and her head held high, crossed the grass and ascended the steps of the terrace.

To her astonishment, every single girl had been provided with a long dress. The gardeners, though a little green about the knees, wore white shirts and bow ties but, as if to demonstrate a pride in their occupation, they had all retained their baize aprons. The musicians sat on a dais between the orange trees with violin, cello and drums, and a haughty lady in a backless evening dress arranged her music on a grand piano.

'But where did it all come from?' Julia gasped.

'All part of the service,' said Gene blandly. 'Come along — we are the leading couple.'

He nodded to the players, who launched into a
dreamy waltz, then led Julia into the centre of the floor
and bowed, holding out his arms. Gliding with him
across the satin-smooth green-and-white-patterned
tiles, Julia hardly noticed the other girls as they joined
the dance with their partners. This, she thought, was the
best day of her life. Probably there would never be
another one to match it, but she didn't care. 'I'll be your
two,' Gene had said — and that's exactly what he was,
completely and magnificently.

143

The dance went on like a long dream, and the glossy leaves of the orange trees rotated slowly against the dazzling glass roof as Julia gazed up, circling delectably with her hand on Gene's shoulder. Tune succeeded tune,

then an interval was declared and the gardeners escorted
the flushed girls to little tables, for ices in silver dishes
and tall glasses of lemonade.

Julia fanned herself with the carved ivory fan as she watched her class-mates chattering and laughing. Unbelievably, Rhona Cheeseman caught her eye from behind the broad shoulders of a young gardener with handsome side whiskers, and gave her a conspiratorial grin and a wink. Julia winked back. As she took the floor again with Gene, this time in a military two-step, she glanced across at Miss Palethorpe, dancing with the Head Gardener, and wondered idly whether Miss Bing was still waiting for the bus. But time had ceased to matter. Arrangements would have been made, she thought easily. No doubt Gene had everything in hand. She must ask him what the E of his surname stood for. It could not be elephant, not for someone so light and skilful on his feet. But the music at that moment changed to a polka, and she had no breath with which to frame her question.

All too soon, it was the last waltz, and then the sad moments of standing still for a few peremptory bars of the National Anthem, after which the musicians briskly packed their instruments away. The gardeners bowed to their partners, escorted them back to the little tables and then walked out through the tall doors, collecting rakes and barrows and hanks of raffia from the terrace, and dispersing down the steps. It was over. The Head Gardener came back and presented Miss Palethorpe with a single white camellia — and then he, too, was gone.

'Leave all borrowed things on the platform beside the piano, please, girls,' called Miss Palethorpe, with her head bent to hide her blushing cheeks as she carefully threaded the silver-wrapped stem of the camellia through the small jet brooch she wore at the neck of her dress.

On the terrace, Julia turned to Gene and said, 'This day has changed my life for ever.'

'Is that good?' he asked gravely.

'Oh, yes!' said Julia. 'It will always be there to remember. I shan't feel so dull any more.'

'My dear,' said Gene, 'you could never be dull.' And he raised her hand to his lips and kissed it.

'I must go and change,' said Julia, seeing the girls begin to assemble in twos on the sweep of gravel below the terrace.

'You'll find the wonderful bag across there,' said Gene, nodding towards the rhododendrons. 'Thank you for bringing it.'

'I didn't know the contents were so exciting,' Julia admitted. She hesitated, then added, 'I'll leave it there. You can make much better use of it than Miss Palethorpe would.' She almost regretted her generosity. It was painful to imagine him dancing with some other girl. She pushed the thought away. 'Thank you — for everything,' she said.

'It was all of your making,' said Gene.

'Julia, do hurry up!' called Miss Palethorpe. 'You'll be late!'

Julia ran across the lawn in her cloud of gauzy tulle, pulling off her gloves. She must not be late. She

wriggled out of the lovely dress, thrust her arms into her school blouse, tugged up the zipper of her navy skirt and trod her feet into their regulation shoes. She placed the satin slippers and the lacy gloves on the open top of the black bin bag, and laid the dress carefully across them, with its rose uppermost. Then she gave a little gasp. The fan! She had left it on the table where she had sat with Gene at the interval. Rhona's wink had made her forget all about it. How stupid!

'*Julia*!' The voice was more strident. 'You *will* be late!'

The fan would have to stay where it was. Gene would find it. Julia snatched up her hat and blazer, ducked under the leathery leaves of the rhododendrons, and started across the lawn.

'*Julia*!' Someone was shaking her, and the voice was close in her ears. 'What are you *doing*? I've called you and called you. If you're going on this outing to the Gardens, you'll have to hurry up or you'll miss the bus.'

Julia's head reeled as she stared at the walls of her room.

'For goodness' sake!' exclaimed her mother. 'What's wrong with you this morning?'

'I don't know,' said Julia. A glance at her bedside clock made her fling back the bedclothes. A few minutes later, she was munching a piece of leathery toast in the kitchen.

'You can't go out with your hair like that,' said her mother.

'Yes, I can,' said Julia calmly. She drank her tepid tea and put on her blazer and hat.

'Well, I think you look a fright,' said her mother. 'But I suppose you can do your hair in the bus on the way to the Gardens. Those things of Auntie's are in a bag by the front door, but don't bother with them if you've got to run.'

'I'm not running,' said Julia. The bag was a shabby canvas holdall with cracked brown plastic reinforcing at its corners. She picked it up and gave her mother a kiss, then walked down the path. When she turned at the gate to wave, her mother was staring after her in perplexity. Julia had never before left the house without her hair in two neat plaits. And she had never been late.

Julia paused by the steps of the Bingo Hall, and put the bag down to unzip it. The musty smell of mothballs rose to make her wrinkle her nose in distaste, and the glass eyes of a balding fur's weasel face stared up. Beneath it, Julia found, were blouses, wool skirts, a felt hat. Not bothering to drag the zipper shut, she left the bag where it was, and walked on. One of the old women who carried her entire household in a dilapidated pram would find it.

Julia had almost wanted to miss the bus but, as in her dream, it was coming down the drive as she reached the school gate. The outing would be nothing but Miss Palethorpe droning on about adjectives. Julia shrank into the shrubs and hoped not to be noticed.

The bus stopped. 'Julia!' the girls were shouting. 'Hello, Jools!' Some of them were banging on the window. The door hissed open. Miss Palethorpe stood at the top of the steps. 'My goodness,' she said, smiling at Julia's tousled hair, 'you are looking very Pre-Raphaelite today. Come along in.' Julia stared up at her, taken aback by the unusual friendliness. Then her heart gave a sudden thump as she saw, pinned under a small jet brooch on the teacher's greyish-mauve dress, a white camellia, with its stem silver-wrapped. 'Sit down quickly,' Miss Palethorpe instructed as the bus moved off again.

Rhona Cheeseman patted the empty seat beside her invitingly. Yesterday, Julia thought, she would have been thrilled. She sat down and leaned her head back against the brown-mottled fabric, trying to sift the conflicting realities. Then Rhona said, 'I was dreaming about you.'

'So was I!' chipped in Margot, leaning over from the seat behind. 'And so was Letitia. It's really funny.'

'They all were,' said Rhona. 'We've been talking about it. You were dancing.' She fished in her pocket and offered Julia a slender packet of lemon-flavoured chewing gum. 'Pretty weird, huh?' she said.

Julia nodded, sliding the wrapper off the gum. She
had never tried it before. Her mother thought chewing
gum was disgusting. 'Wait till you hear about *my*
dream,' she said. And, chewing enjoyably, she told
Rhona all about it.

'Wow,' breathed Rhona at the end of the recital.
'And Miss Paleface really *is* wearing a camellia! You're
not making it up?'

'Cross my heart,' vowed Julia.

'*We* didn't see this bloke who looked like Robin
Hood,' piped up Letitia, who had been listening from
the seat behind.

'Neither did I,' said Rhona, looking suspiciously at
Julia. 'It was just you, doing these fabulous dances, all
on your own. Miss P. was bowled over. And this guy
was called Gene, you said?'

'That's right,' said Julia. 'At first, he said just to call
him Mr E., but then —'

Rhona shouted with laughter. 'Mr E? *Mystery*? Who
are you kidding? Dead brilliant, though — I'd never
have thought of that.'

Julia blushed. Had Gene simply been teasing her, knowing she wouldn't see the pun? She tried again. 'Well, anyway, he said I could call him Gene. I thought it sounded like a girl's name, but he said it was like Gene Kelly.'

'Only it was Gene E!' spluttered Rhona, almost choking with amusement. 'The genie of the lamp, I suppose!'

This further gem of Julia's invention was passed round the bus, causing snorts of mirth.

'Dunno why I got you so wrong,' said Rhona, shaking her head. 'I'd written you off as dull.'

Julia smiled. The sudden popularity was wonderful, but Gene, genie-like, had disappeared in a cloud of bad jokes, leaving a terrible emptiness. The white flower Miss Palethorpe wore on her dress meant nothing. Just a coincidence. 'It was all of your making,' Gene had said.

'I like your hair like that,' Rhona said when she had recovered from her amusement. 'Suits you.'

'Makes a change,' said Julia. She stared out at the passing trees. Despite all reason, a wild hope remained that Gene would be at the Botanic Gardens to meet them.

When the bus slowed down, the sight of the tall, wrought-iron gates made Julia so breathless that she could not move, but sat pleating a chewing-gum wrapper between her fingers while the other girls poured out. 'No point in hurrying,' Rhona agreed, marooned on the window side of her as Julia had been marooned by the black plastic bin bag.

He was not there. The disappointment was overwhelming. The girls lined up in twos, and Rhona fell in beside Julia so that a thin girl called Celia Tripp had to walk on her own. They made their way past the formal beds of geraniums and the floral clock. The sun was hidden behind lowering grey clouds, solid as clay, and a chill wind blew a spatter of raindrops across the gravel. The dream was most dreadfully perverted. Grieving for the lost beauty of it all, Julia walked beside Rhona to the Cold House.

'Now,' said Miss Palethorpe, 'in here, I want you to imagine what life must be like in a cold, inhospitable terrain.' Was it imagination, or did her watery blue eyes rest on Julia with a kind of hope? The girls were giggling and nudging each other, watching Julia. She scowled down at her feet as Miss Palethorpe led the way in. An empty crisps bag skittered slowly across the concrete floor in the draught from the white-painted metal door.

'Bleak,' said Miss Palethorpe. 'Challenging.' The girls shuffled and sniffed. Julia stared at a small tuft of lichen. Rain dotted the roof of the Cold House with transparent circles. 'If you have all taken careful note of this atmosphere,' Miss Palethorpe said, 'we will proceed to the Tropical House.' And she tied the strings of a plastic rain-hat under her chin.

Rhona, with her hands thrust into the pockets of her jacket, leaned against the wall beside Julia until the

others had all gone out. Then she said, 'Let's go and have a cup of coffee. The old bat will never notice we're not in the Tropical House — she'll think we're behind a banana tree or something.'

'Okay,' said Julia. 'They'll be in there for ages — it's lovely and warm.' Boiling, Gene had said. Following Rhona through an evasive manoeuvre round a weeping ash tree, she found herself running across the lawn towards the Orangery, outside which a notice said, Refreshments. They pushed open the tall glass door. The leafiness of the interior was overlaid by the residual smells of stale tea and of many people wearing their outdoor clothes.

'I'll get it,' said Rhona, fishing in her purse as she approached the counter where a woman lethargically wrapped sandwiches in cling-film. 'You find a table,' she added over her shoulder.

Since the place was completely empty, there was plenty of choice. Ghostly music echoed in Julia's head as she looked up at the orange trees and remembered how their glossy leaves had circled against the glass with her waltzing. Gene had led her past the statue of the stooping nymph to the table under the tree whose branches were studded with green, marble-sized tangerines.

The tiny fruits were there, just as they had been in the dream, but Julia cautioned herself against romantic imaginings. The presence of the little tangerines did not

158

mean anything, any more than did Miss Palethorpe's camellia. She must be sensible. The dream had been lovely, but this was the true reality, her hand pulling out the chair and feeling the scrape of its legs across the floor.

Then a shiver of shock ran down her spine and made her heart thump suddenly in her chest. There, at her feet, slim and pale against the green-and-white-patterned tiles, lay the carved ivory fan.

Julia bent and picked it up, spreading its delicate blades against the palm of her hand and staring down at its intricate patterning. She sat down, still gazing at it, and felt her lips curve in a smile of pure happiness.

'You look cheerful!' Rhona called as she approached with a tray.

'I am,' said Julia. Under cover of the table's edge, she folded the fan and slipped it into her blazer pocket. Perhaps she would tell Rhona about it, but she was not quite sure yet.

Rhona looked suspiciously at Julia's flushed face as she put the tray down. 'What are you up to?' she demanded.

'I just feel happy,' said Julia, and pulled a chair out for her friend. 'It's having a two,' she explained, and laughed at the richness of the words.

'Yeah,' agreed Rhona. 'Rotten being on your own, isn't it. I got chocolate biccies. Hope you like them.'

'Lovely,' said Julia. 'My turn next time.'

The days lay enticingly ahead, full of wild possibilities, and she could not stop smiling.